Sissci

A Hands of Death Novel

R.L. Parker

For the members of the Fantasy Writers Club discord.
You are an inspiration. I can't thank you enough.
Stay awesome.

Timeline / Reading List

-6500 BGA - All Hail the New Gods (novel, coming soon)

-69 BGA - The Curse of Kishina (short story)

575 1st Era - Threads of Night (short story)

575 1st Era - Siscci

575 1st Era - Dusk (novel, coming soon)

113 2nd Era - Bathed in the Blood of Ravens

114 2nd Era - Enveloped by Dark's Embrace (coming soon)

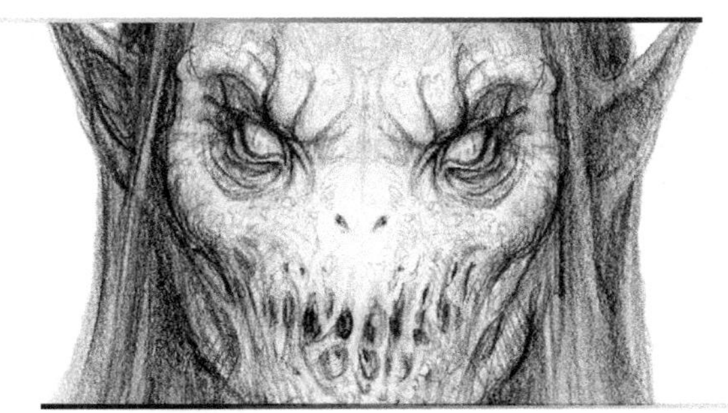

Prologue:
Threads of Night

Ris'Enliss, Amaethur 12th, 575 of the 1st Era

SORSCHA DOUBLED over in pain, grasping her head as if it were about to explode. The other passengers barged past her, seemingly unconcerned with her affliction. They'd been trapped with her aboard the Daring Faun for days and had witnessed her episodes enough to pay them no heed... something she sorely wished she was capable of herself. When the pain subsided, she found herself alone on the docks.

In years past Port Gandraias would have been bustling with activity, but from Sorscha's position on the docks the town seemed nearly vacant, if not abandoned. Six of the city's seven docks stood empty. No dock workers had emerged to help unload the Daring Faun, and the ship's crew had already gone ashore and vanished into the dark city streets.

In recent years, the majority of the kingdom's trade had slowly shifted to land routes controlled by the warring fiefdoms in the south. Their constant shifts in power resulted in price wars to win Tellrindosian business, as exports were a primary source of income for the war ravaged nobles. Shipping goods to the north past unpredictable armies, through pirate infested waters, became too expensive an operation, by comparison.

Trade had shifted to accommodate the times; leaving Port Gandraias struggling, and driving many of its citizens to more profitable locations.

Her arrival at such an underutilized port had been intentional. With her business in Pelrigoss complete, she'd set sail to Port Gandraias expecting precisely those circumstances. She needed to speak to her master, and that meant avoiding as much distraction as possible. The nature of her mission had meant her welcome in Pelrigoss was at an end, and neither the Kingdom of Haern nor the 'Warlunds' to the south were viable options for her task.

She studied the city for a brief moment as a dull throb returned, sending sharp pains through her left eye. Such pain had become part of her daily life, but the episodes were rarely this frequent. She wasn't sure if the escalation was his doing or not, but she intended to ask.

Am I not a faithful servant? Do I need such reminders of my responsibilities?

Her challenge for the evening would be finding a place where she could commune uninterrupted. What she was, and what she intended to do, wasn't particularly savory to the public. Being a Witch wasn't against the law, but simple folk often treated her like a criminal once they discovered her nature.

Those that knew the truth stayed clear of their own accord, but she was in unfamiliar territory. Unless she planned to traipse around town, boldly declaring herself as the 'Night Witch', hoping her reputation had preceded her, discretion was her only option.

She briefly pondered whether or not she could make it out of town to the small caves to the south. Suddenly, a familiar sensation emerged at the back of her mind, slowly increasing in intensity.

I'll have to do it here... this isn't ideal, but I don't know how much longer I can last. I need answers.

Growing more frustrated with each passing second, she descended the ramp off the docks and into the city streets. She hurried as fast as her old bones would let her, intent on finding a safe place from which to perform her ritual.

The warehouses, office buildings, and small businesses closest to the docks had been boarded shut for several years and had been slowly weathered by the cold, salty air. There was no doubt in her mind she could easily gain entry to the building of her choosing, but being arrested for breaking into a vacant building was the type of attention she was trying to avoid.

She gripped her cane more firmly and paused for a moment as her vision blurred; her face contorting as the sensation yet again washed through her mind.

Be patient, foul demon. You'll get your answers faster if you let me walk for five minutes without the unnecessary interruptions!

Struggle as she might, she couldn't recall a time before the recurring pains. Were the pains present before her pact with Vaxtra, or had they only surfaced after she signed the contract? The only thing she could be certain of was that the agony that once again swelled within her mind was far more intense than it had ever been.

When she regained her composure, she continued at a slower, more methodical pace. Heading west along the first row of buildings toward the far end of town, she studied the sights, sounds, and smells about her. The faint sound of music and chatter echoed between the buildings to the north. Hints of overly seasoned barley stew accompanied the cool night breeze.

She rounded the corner to see the Argyle Elk Tavern on the far corner of the next intersection. A tavern wasn't an ideal location for a ritual, but unless she wanted to commandeer someone's home she was out of options. Begrudgingly, she gripped her cane with purpose and gave in to her circumstances.

The tavern was bustling with activity, its noise and the stench of the patrons' recreational substances reached her well before she arrived at the door. Located on the farthest end of the longest street near the docks, few locals dared approach the establishment, let alone walk in.

Even with the preferable collection of unsavory travelers and sailors as its only patrons, no tavern was appropriate for what she planned to do. Biting back on her hesitation, she pushed the swinging doors open and stepped inside.

The tavern's interior offered little in the way of improvement compared to the chilly night air outside. Small, table-top candles were the only source of light, which she supposed was wise considering the rowdy clientele. Rectangular holes in the exterior walls hinted at where windows had once been; long ago broken and never replaced.

She made her way through the crowd as a cool breeze passed through the building, candle flames fluttering in its wake. Two colorfully dressed men played music at one end of the bar, standing on small crates so that all could see... not that anyone was paying attention to them.

Most of the patrons yelled louder than normal, trying to be heard over the sound of a poorly played flute and the haphazard banging of a drum. The musicians played harder, trying to break through the din, driving crowd noise even higher from their efforts. The combination bode well for her plans, and her chances of being interrupted seemed slim.

Perhaps this won't go as poorly as I expected.

She hobbled directly behind the bar, without pause or concern, and approached the bartender without being noticed. He was a tall, burly man; more than capable of defending his tavern should a patron take things too far.

A quick tug on his vest sent him spinning toward her. Seeing a grown man, of his size and stature, with such a stark look of surprise on his face brought her joy.

"I need a room, good sir," she explained.

"You can't be back here!" he yelled.

"What?" she asked loudly, pretending she hadn't heard him.

He grumbled angrily, wrinkled his face in frustration and escorted her into the kitchen. Following closely behind her, he wasn't able to see the smirk on her face.

Once they arrived, he closed the door and turned to face her angrily.

"What!" he yelled, seeking her purpose for going behind the bar.

"What?" she asked feebly, in the weakest, most elderly voice she could muster.

"I don't have time for thi–"

"I need a room on the top floor," she pleaded.

"You barged behind my bar for that?"

"My old bones need rest, and the noise is just so overwhelming. Can you put me up in the farthest room from the bar?"

"The farthest room from the bar is at the Gandraias Inn, sixteen blocks north. Go, and leave me be... and stay out of my bar!"

"Oh, I don't think I can make it that far... not with all these coins weighing me down," she whimpered.

"Nice try, now get ou–"

She jingled the bag that hung at her hip to interrupt him.

"I really do need sleep, kind sir. I can pay... I'm no vagrant. I would've stopped at the old Dirkish, but they seem to have closed. I already had to walk all the way here from the docks... alone... in the dark. Would you make an old woman walk sixteen blocks to find a pillow?"

"Fine! Six silver. I only *have* one room left, and it's the most expensive."

A cook barged past him and through the door to deliver a plate of food. No sooner did the door open than the sound of breaking glass echoed through the kitchen. The bartender gripped his hand towel so hard his knuckles went white.

"Could you be a dear and help me up the stairs? These old bo–"

"Let's get this over with!"

∴ ∴ ∴

THE ROOM the proprietor brought her to was quaint, if she'd ever seen such a thing. Situated on the third floor, it was just far enough away to ignore the din below, but not so far as to pretend it didn't exist.

After a quick look around to ensure it was large enough for her needs, she turned back to her escort.

"Could you remove the bed?" she asked, smiling feebly. Knowing her request was unusual, she leaned heavily on her cane and presented the confused man with the saddest look she could muster. "These old bones are so used to the ground... you'd be doing me a kindness."

"Why don't you just sleep on the floor beside the bed, then?" he countered.

He could hear the beginnings of a fight brewing downstairs, and his patience was gone.

"Oh, I wouldn't want to trip over it in the middle of the night when nature calls... I'd ruin your floor! I don't want to be a burden," she said, feigning concern.

"Like I said before, the Gandraias Inn is–"

"An extra ten silver for your troubles," she offered.

She smiled again, pleadingly, hoping to play on his sensitivities.

"Fine!" he barked as a crashing sound rang out from below. "I don't have time for this... Bertrum will be up shortly to remove it," he finished with a sigh.

She listened as the man barged down the stairs, yelling for his patrons to stop destroying the tavern. With a sigh, she made her way to the back wall and leaned against it to wait for Bertrum. By the sounds of the tussle below, his arrival would take some time.

The nagging sensation returned at the back of her mind, increasing in intensity until she could stand no more. She dropped her cane and hunched over, hands cupping her face. It was all she could do to avoid screaming in agony.

Gasping, she dropped to her knees as the pain finally subsided.

Vaxtra better have answers!

Dropping back onto her rear, she closed her eyes and thought back to her pact with Vaxtra trying to remember the specific words he'd used.

There has to be a clue.

The memories escaped her. She could sense that the event had occurred. She could feel it at the back of her mind. The memory was right there, within reach... but she couldn't access it.

The pact was real; she'd served her master for far too long for it not to be, so why couldn't she remember agreeing to serve?

When she finally opened her eyes, the bed was gone and she realized she'd never noticed Bertrum's arrival. She'd been so lost in her thoughts, she'd missed both the bed's removal and the closing of her door.

It wasn't like her to be so unaware.

How long have I been sitting here?

With the bed gone, the room was all but empty. The small bits of furniture that still lined the walls would be inconsequential. Of critical importance was that she now had the floor space to do what she needed to do; commune with Vaxtra.

She grabbed her cane, braced herself, and pushed off the floor with all her might. Standing was such a trivial thing, often taken for granted by the young. She couldn't remember being young, and and the act was far from trivial for her.

Her age was yet another in a series of mysteries she hoped to resolve.

Sighing at herself for the distraction, she brought her mind back to the task at hand. She moved to the center of the room and carefully lowered herself to the floor again, using the cane for leverage. Once seated, she leaned to the side and placed the cane at the end of her reach.

One by one, she removed six pieces of quartz crystal from the pouch hidden beneath her robe and placed them in her lap. She then retrieved a small piece of charcoal and carefully drew sigils on the surrounding floor, encircling herself.

Leaning forward, she drew a similar ring in front of her, then connected them with two lines of runes. Her drawings complete, she placed a piece of quartz behind her and one at each of her sides. Finally, she placed the remaining three crystals around the smaller circle to form an opposing triangle.

With the ritual space prepared, she closed her eyes and sank deep into a meditative trance; preparing to reach out to her demonic lord.

∴ ∴ ∴

A DEATHLY calm radiated from the core of Sorscha's being. She could hear nothing but her thoughts, and slowly they too grew silent. Her mind pushed aside everything except for her breathing and her heartbeat. She then bent both to her will, slowing them to within an inch of her own death.

She reached into the room with her mind; stretching further and further with each successive beat of her heart. Pulling with her will, she drew upon the shadows. As each pulse of her heart sent blood coursing through her veins, it pulled darkness toward the crystals.

The umbral forces pulsed in waves, surging towards the crystals like ripples in a pond; flowing in reverse, pulsating in sync with her heartbeat.

Smokey, black tendrils drew into the crystals, their milky white structures turning black as ink.

The room brightened as her power sapped the room of light's opposing force. When the room grew as radiant as the sun, her eyes shot open and a deep breath escaped her lips like a hiss.

Pure, primal darkness poured from the gems, following the lines of runes, and passing through each crystal in its path.

With each circuit the powers grew stronger, thicker and taller until the sigils underneath were no longer visible.

The crystals rose into the air, hovering inches above the swirling darkness.

The room grew brighter still.

"Diem noch, th'rul... Vaxtra! Aeg vog, ve'el thu Malthax! Diem noch Vaxtra!" chanted Sorscha, repeating the words she'd used so many times before. Her voice sounded hollow, as if she were devoid of life.

The shadows circling the small circle of runes reached up and coalesced.

Red, scaly skin came into view.

Yellow, slanted eyes with thin black lines for pupils peered through the shadowy cluster of power, piercing into her being.

"What news have you?" asked the apparition. Its voice was deep and resonating; shaking the floor as it spoke.

"The Tryn shaman has been cursed. She knew nothing of the gate," she answered.

"Then you have failed me! Again!" growled Vaxtra.

"It is not I that have failed. It is you. Your agents supplied you with–"

"Such insolence!" yelled Vaxtra.

"I serve you willingly, yet you act on unfounded claims like a reckless child. I do not beg for your approval. I do not grovel at your feet. You are so consumed with this mysterious 'gate' that you fail to question the information your pathetic, useless agents bring to you!

"You have but one faithful servant, and you dare punish me with your psychic assaults when I am but a minute late in–"

"I am the source of your power. If I sought to punish you, would I not just take that which keeps you alive? That which you embrace? That which you hold so dear?" he challenged.

"You are not the source of these pains?" she asked.

"What pains?" asked Vaxtra.

She took advantage of the moment and drew upon Vaxtra's full power. He screamed in rage as his essence streamed through the air between them. He attempted in vain to withdraw from their commune, but her sigils held fast.

Reaching out with her mind, she used Vaxtra's power to draw shadows from the rest of the tavern, and the night beyond. The entire block brightened as she deprived the area of darkness, glowing like a beacon in the night sky.

She pushed the power deep into the recesses of her mind, seeking to break whatever barrier was preventing access to her memories. Perhaps behind the barrier was the answer, or the secrets to a cure for her pain. Perhaps the answer lay in her pact with Vaxtra, and the terms of that pact which she could no longer recall.

As the barrier cracked, the world returned to normal. Shadows crashed back into place with a sound like thunder. The impact of the sudden return to darkness threw witnesses off their feet, out of beds, and out of chairs for hundreds of yards.

Sorscha gasped in pain as the barrier fell, and the memories of thousands of years confronted her all at once.

∴ ∴ ∴

SHE LAY *dying on the ground as battle raged all around her, staring up at a sea of weeping eyes. Her tribe's men screamed and moaned all around her, their lives were lost and she could do nothing to save them. She could feel the essence of her being draining from her. At least she would serve a purpose in death... she would contribute to the circle of life... that was enough.*

Energy surged through her, rising from the ground. She didn't understand what was happening. Confusion! Pain! So much pain she couldn't breathe! Was she breathing? Had she stopped? This didn't make any-

She forced the vision from her mind, gasping.

How long ago was-

Another vision flooded her mind, breaking her train of thought.

A great army dotted the horizon, standing in formation, ready to attack. Thousands of years had passed since she was reborn. Thousands of years preventing wars, thwarting conflict, and protecting the innocent peoples of the lands. Would it all end now? Were her efforts in vain? Had her involvement in human affairs caused an escalation?

She had to act. Squabbles between city states were one thing, but this... this sight before her meant war. Pure... unadulterated war. How had she missed it, and... who was this? Two beings in the middle of their line. Two beings like she-

The vision faded abruptly. She tried desperately to grasp its meaning, but the next vision came too quickly.

Somehow she'd known of the elves. In six-thousand years she'd never seen one, but somehow she'd always known. Here they were, standing before her, pleading for aid. Somehow she knew they shared blood. She wanted answers. More pressing issues prevailed. The elves were in danger. Nay, their planet Àl arha was in danger... as was Ea-

Gasping, she fell backward.

Elves? But I already know about elves... and what's Àl arha? What did I mean by danger? What danger-

The sudden arrival of another vision made it feel as if her chest was about to burst open.

For years she'd work with the other two Elder Ones to save humanity from itself. Now on the precipice of worldwide destruction, one of them had broken their accord. Jealousy. Rage. Greed. He radiated the very things they'd fought to overcome, the very things they'd tried to teach mankind to abandon. Who were they, if not a beacon of hope?

Surely they were not gods. Did he think himself such? Was that his desire? Pain ripped through her as his spell tore flesh from bone, rendering her nearly to ash. She stood in defiance, willing her flesh to grow back, and blasted him with the whole of her power.

He did not fall. He smiled back at her, wickedly. Something had changed. He was the third of their kind, and the weakest. How had he become so strong?

The images of the two men rushed through her mind too quickly to discern their appearances, but she could feel who they were, and feel a connection to them. One of them had meant quite a lot to her.

I am an Elder One? What does that mean? Who was–

An endless stream of memories flooded her mind in rapid succession.

Someone had cursed her to wander the world, protecting great seals of power. Seals that stole magic from her world and siphoned it into another. Seals that, if broken, would mean the destruction of everything and everyone.

For nearly five-thousand years she served, living a decade at a time near each seal. Every ten years the seals moved her to the next seal against her will. She lost her memory with each transition and slowly regained it during her stay, only to repeat the cycle again.

Nearly five-hundred fragments of memories flooded her, one after another. Societies rising, societies falling, world wars, invasions, advancements she couldn't comprehend... at the end, everything had been for naught. It was humanity that broke the seals and caused the destruction of their own world.

The power was ripping her apart, nay, it was ripping the entire planet apart. It was ripping them both apart, for they were one. She drew upon every ounce of power she or the planet could provide. She had to hold the world together just a little longer. The evacuation was almost complete!

He would save them. He had to save them. She had to give him more ti–

Sorscha screamed louder than her voice alone should have allowed. Unbridled power welled up from within, as if released along with her memories.

She was standing on a new world now. How much time had passed? Where was she? Who... was she? Her memory was gone. A being approached. The twelve foot tall, red-scaled being knelt before her. His black horns glistened in the orange light of the world's star. His yellow eyes pierced her inner being, seeing through her.

He terrified her.

"You needn't be afraid, girl. I am here to offer you power... power to save yourself from this place... power to set me free," he explained. His voice made the ground tremble, but his tone put her at ease. He placed one massive hand on her shoulder, saying, "I am Vaxtra, Prince of-"

"Vaxtra! I met him on his home world!" she gasped.

Even free of the vision, she could still feel the weight of his hand, the heat of his breath and the ground trembling as he spoke.

The cataclysm took my memory, and he exploited my weakness to lay claim to me.

She didn't need his power. She *was* power. She could feel it deep inside her.

It is he that draws power from me!

She opened her mind, reaching out to Vaxtra with her will.

I am Sorscha, the first of the Elder Ones. I will not be bound by you!

With every ounce of her will, and her rediscovered power, she pushed to break free of their bond.

∴ ∴ ∴

VAXTRA HAD taught her the ways of sorcery and witchcraft. For decades she'd lived on his world, learning to draw upon shadow and darkness. He had led her to believe that their pact granted her power. She'd been too weak at the time to understand the truth.

'Sorcery,' he had explained, *'bears limitations. You must consume a source of power to cast your spells. Thus, the power of a sorceress depends on the abundance of her source. Since I have taught you to harness the power of darkness and draw from the shadows... your power will be without limit!'*

She'd met Vaxtra nearly three-thousand years ago; a fact that was now clear with the return of her memories. Through him, she had learned to master both Sorcery and Channeling. For the one she drew upon shadows, and for the other she drew upon him.

Neither source of power lie within her.

As a sorceress, her powers were unmatched. She had traveled the whole of Ayrelon in Vaxtra's service and had met no one as powerful as she. This power that rose within her was different... it was inside of her, generated by her own being; her soul. She could feel it within her, begging for release.

Once again, she pulled upon the shadows with her will, drawing their power inside her. She channeled Vaxtra, leeching his powers, pulling them within her and combining the two into one. Letting those powers continue to stream into her being, she reached down inside, seeking the forces that grew therein.

Unbridled energies poured into her consciousness, intertwined with the shadows and the demonic. As the powers neared a strength she could barely contain, she realized another force was waiting just beyond her reach.

It felt familiar.

It invited her to partake.

Memories rushed in as she touched the power she'd sensed. The fourth power crashed into her body, raw and uncontrollable.

It was a force which she'd long ago learned to harness; a force she'd long ago forgotten she could. As the primal forces of Life and Death rushed into her, she combined them with the others.

With a strength he had deprived her of for centuries, she channeled the combined magical forces toward Vaxtra across the planes of existence with every ounce of her being.

Vaxtra calmly laughed at her attempt, slamming the ethereal link between them closed; forcing the energies to go elsewhere.

Raw magical forces splashed back into Sorscha, throwing her through the window and down into the street. The powers of shadow, life, death, her soul, and her demonic host blasted through everything within a hundred yards.

The Argyle Elk shattered violently. Shards of wood, iron, and glass rained down across several city blocks.

Sorscha struggled to stand. Her entire body was in pain. Her brain felt as if it were melting.

Chaos flooded her mind; carried by memories no living soul should experience. Eons of torture piled into her in an instant. The memories were foreign, twisted, and confused; as if their source didn't understand how to convey them.

She felt the misery of her world; the suffering as two worlds violently merged in dimensional collapse. Still bound to its essence, she became the world's conduit; it's memory; it's voice.

As her mind flailed, anxiously attempting to control and understand the flood of memories and emotions, she lashed out.

"No more!" she screamed as energy burst forth from her chest.

She had absorbed most of the energy deflected by Vaxtra, and in her weakened state of mind she could no longer contain it.

Shadows seeped out of her flesh, enveloping her arms. Long tendrils grew from her fists as she screamed in pain. She no longer knew if the pain was hers, or the memories of the world's demise which plagued her.

She reached for her face as magical tears seared a path down her cheeks.

Several citizens had rushed to the scene, trying to determine what was going on. The movement of her arms sent the tendrils whipping through the air, slicing several bystanders in half.

Screams of terror reached through the pain, drawing her temporarily back into the moment. Her eyes shot open, black with her power.

Her decrepit form straightened and drew upright.

She couldn't comprehend the destruction before her; the shards of buildings, the piles of dust, the pieces of corpses or the shrieking citizens. Her mind was no longer her own.

Sorscha moved her right arm slowly, lifting her hand into the air.

Guards raced toward her from all directions, many raised from their slumber and half dressed.

Citizens fled down the streets, pouring out of their homes in terror.

She raised her palm toward the sky and slowly curled her fingers inward.

Thin streams of ash rose from the surrounding area, crossed the distance to her and collected in her raised palm.

The guards' eyes grew wide in horror at the sight. Many attempted to flee.

As she slowly closed her hand into a fist, her knuckles popped like snapping twigs.

She turned her hand over as the rest of the guards second-guessed their approach.

It was already too late.

Sorscha opened her outstretched hand, letting the dust and

ash fall toward the ground.

Every living thing in Port Gandraias instantly turned to ash.

∴ ∴ ∴

SORSCHA'S MIND slowly returned to normal.

The flood of memories slowed to a trickle and then stopped.

She wasn't sure how long she'd stood there, lost in a haze of confused rage. The only thing she was certain of was her true identity... and her newfound purpose.

Small piles of ash encircled her. More piles lay down every street as far as she could see. The air smelled of death and decay.

The area was still brighter than it should have been; the shadows had not yet reclaimed it.

Her body returned to its normal, decrepit state as she wept. She wept not for the loss of life, but for the futility of everything she'd ever done to save humanity. She wept for the time she'd wasted, and the time she'd lost.

She looked around for her cane, but could not find it.

Hunching as she walked, she stumbled through the streets looking for a substitute. Finding a table leg from the tavern, she sighed and settled into her circumstances.

That was when she remembered.

Her life was not the only thing forgotten.

"Kahnel," she said in recognition, then shook her head. "Kane," she corrected, remembering further.

He was the Elder One who had rebelled and fought against her. It was he that inspired the events that led to the breaking of the seals. Kane had taken her memories on Melthax, causing her to meet and make a pact with Vaxtra.

Kane was coming to Ayrelon. It was he that sought the gate.

"Not this time," she muttered.

Slowly she walked out of the city, plotting and scheming. She remembered all of her past, even if the memories had come at great cost. It was time for her to leverage that past to protect Ayrelon from Kane; a man who could kill Ayrelon's gods.

The forces of good alone would stand no chance. All her life she had been 'good', and where had that gotten her? Where had that gotten the world?

No, *I must find balance... I must* cause *balance. Only balance can defeat him. Only balance can save mortals from themselves.*

'*What is evil anyway, if not a simple matter of perspective?*' she'd once been asked. Those words resonated with her now.

With a new perspective and a newfound purpose, she left the city and walked south. She cast her mind back to the man who had uttered those words. He'd uttered many things to her back in those times. He had known things he couldn't have known, seen things he couldn't have seen, and done things no man could do.

He had questioned her reality and tried to convince her to be someone else. The man had pleaded with her to change her ways, or rather, not become something he feared. It was as if he knew she'd become what she had just become, eons before it happened.

She decided to take heed of his pleas, but not for the reasons he desired. Instead, she would use the information laced within his words to affect change; to manipulate the world and push toward the only thing that could help its people defeat Kane.

A balance had to be struck.

Heroes need to rise... on both sides.

Nations must be founded.

The sword must be reclaimed.

Kingdoms must fall.

The son of a god must be slain by his brother.

She had a lot of work to do. A particular Toor was waiting to meet her, though it would be decades before he was born. Nevertheless, she had a mission now, and Vaxtra was but a nuisance. They were still bound, and that would need to be addressed. However, after her display, she was certain he would bother her no more.

I will deal with him later.

As she walked into the darkness, into the wilds beyond the city, she thanked the man who had set her upon her path. Without his interference, she might still be lost.

"Thank you, Mordechai. We will meet soon enough."

SISCCI
A HANDS OF DEATH NOVEL

FOREBODING

ANOTHER TEAR caressed her cheek as she watched in horror at her master's whip snapping against the already-broken skin of her would-be brother's back. She wanted nothing more than to break free and put an end to his torture; knowing that unlocking their shackles would be the simple part. Stopping Johorr's violent outburst and then caring for Thomlin during their escape, and likely his entire life thereafter... the sheer prospect of such a responsibility overwhelmed her.

Her subconscious mind screamed out for her to stand up and declare that it had all been her fault; she'd broken Johorr's favorite tankard, not Thomlin. Returning to the campfire from the rear of the carriage with his dinner and ale delicately balanced on her arms had been her decision, not his.

I should have made trips! I could have watched where I was stepping!

After traveling as Johorr's slave for over twenty years, she knew better than to succumb to her internal desires. Claiming the burden of guilt would only lead to two bleeding slaves; both under-performing because of their pain and heading directly down the path toward even more beatings. There was simply no reasoning with Johorr when he was enraged.

She knew it was best for them both if she kept her mouth shut. Thomlin knew it as well, and his eyes said as much as their gaze met across the camp. As the whip ripped through his already tattered shirt—tearing at his flesh as it had so many times before—he looked at Syl'Kara and smiled. It was a forced smile; barely more than a grimace as he bit back against the pain.

Thomlin couldn't speak. He was born with a defect that prevented him from producing anything more than the simple hiss of rushing air. His silence often compounded Johorr's rage, driving him to whip harder and longer in some feeble attempt to make the boy wail. Thomlin couldn't wail. He couldn't protest. All he could do was take the beating in silence; and he had plenty of experience doing so.

Syl'Kara looked out for Thomlin as best she could in their day-to-day lives. He saw it as his responsibility to take Johorr's beatings for her whenever the opportunity presented itself. She knew that about him, and knew that it didn't upset him that she hadn't spoken up about the broken tankard's true cause. It was his duty to be her whipping boy, and in his mind, it was one of the few things he was good for.

When Johorr finished, he tossed the whip haphazardly at Syl'Kara, demanding, "Put that away and fetch my ale, ya good-fer-nuthin' welp!"

She wiped the tears from her cheeks and stood, carefully coiling the whip like she knew he preferred. After stowing it in the satchel that was sitting by his hip, she returned to the rear of the carriage with a simple mug and once again tapped the small keg. Carefully watching her step, and the balance in her arms, she deftly traversed the camp and avoided the small cluster of roots she'd tripped over on her previous attempt, right next to Thomlin's bedroll.

"Here is your evening ale, my lord. Would you like anything else?" she asked meekly as she handed him the frothy mug.

"Silence! I must contemplate our route!" he belted, taking a large tug on his drink.

She could have said his words along with him, had she felt snarky. He said the same thing every night when she asked after his needs. He expected her to ask, and if she didn't, he'd have whipped her just like Thomlin. So, she asked. Nightly. Even though he never once had any further desires.

Thomlin lay on his belly, staring at Johorr with anger in his eyes while she tended the wounds on his back. She'd seen him suffer worse beatings, if she was being honest. Those beatings usually happened less frequently, however.

Two nights in a row, she lamented as she dabbed more ointment onto Thomlin's tattered skin. He winced ever-so-slightly at her touch. *I wish he'd take us south already. Just a little closer to Haern, and I can break us free. Does he know that to be my plan? Is that why he keeps us in the frozen north?*

Sleep did not come easily for either of them that night. Johorr passed out just as he always did, his belly full of ale and his mind devoid of regret.

.∴ .∴ .∴

A STRANGE sound echoed through the forest in the dead of night, intruding on Syl'Kara's tenuous grasp on the dreaming world. She quickly opened her eyes, terrified that whatever caused the disturbance might come barreling through the trees at any moment and decimate their camp.

The sound of it reminded her of a demonstration she'd seen on a previous trip to Gusarski Cove many years before. A captain had brought his ship to port to have new weaponry installed. Johorr and Syl'Kara stood on shore with the man, having just delivered the last ingredients he needed to make the device function. As proof of the authenticity of their goods, the weapon was test fired—once— aimed toward the sea.

It was an experimental canon, designed to attack nearby shores, or so the captain had bragged. When he gave the signal and the weapon fired, the explosion was so loud and terrifying that Syl'Kara involuntarily ducked to the ground, covered her ears and gently wept.

She was much older now, and not as prone to such moments of weakness; though the scenario before her caused a great deal of concern. Her entire body was tense, and the tiny hairs on the back of her neck were tingling. Something was wrong; she could feel it in the air. There was an electricity to it as if lightning would strike at any moment, but the sky was completely clear.

Taking care not to drag her leg chains across the ground and wake Johorr, she stood up and studied the forest and the night sky above. Nothing seemed out of place, and there was no movement beyond the first line of trees. Being part Dynar—a race of elves that favored nocturnal activity—she had far superior night vision than anyone else she'd ever met. Not only could she see no signs of movement, she could hear no evidence of nearby animal activity. Her concern quickly rose to a state of alarm.

She was about to wake Thomlin—out of fear that he wouldn't have time to prepare for an attack—when the night sky to the north suddenly grew many times brighter than day. The glow emanated from a point in the distance, far beyond her ability to identify. It grew quickly into what seemed to be a dome of light, reaching into the sky from beyond the forest to the north.

Is that Port Gandraias?

Just as quickly as it appeared, the light dissipated as if comprised of smoke, slowly swirling into the sky before vanishing entirely. Another sound accompanied the visual effect, which she couldn't explain. Instead of an explosion, it sounded more like the hiss of fresh meat sizzling atop a fire, but more abrupt and short-lived.

The sounds of animals fleeing the distant event rang out through the trees. Several deer frantically ran through the clearing past their camp, heading south toward safety. She stood for a time, hand half-outstretched toward Thomlin, staring at the northern sky, terrified that something was coming for them.

After what seemed like hours, she finally calmed enough to take a seat next to the smoldering campfire. She added two fresh logs and stoked the flame back to life with a few well-placed puffs of air. Once the fire sprang to life, she sat with her back to it and brought her legs up toward her chest, wrapping her arms around her knees.

She didn't normally sleep, at least not like humans did. More often than not, she simply meditated or slipped into a state halfway between dreaming and waking. It was normal for her to be the only one awake. Night was the only time she had to herself; something she usually looked forward to.

That wasn't the case in recent weeks, however. She was going through what she assumed was her final growth spurt. Every few years she'd sleep deeply every night for a few weeks, or months, and would grow a few inches. She knew from the few elves she'd seen in their travels that they rarely came much taller than she already was. There was no way to know how much longer the growth spurt would last, or how much taller she would grow. The only thing she was sure of was that it exhausted her beyond reason—in a way that was very unfamiliar to adult elves—and that whatever had just happened was going to haunt her dreams if she attempted to rest.

Dawn couldn't come quickly enough. Even though she knew

the coming day meant doing menial tasks for a man who refused to do anything for himself, and clinging to the side of a carriage he forbade her from riding in for hours on end... it would still be a welcome reprieve from the fear that was slowly overtaking her.

She quietly hummed a simple song that her first adoptive mother once sang to her. The song irritated Johorr, so she often avoided humming it. He was asleep, and she needed the comfort that her memories of it provided. She missed Geela in moments of distress; more than she cared to admit.

∴ ∴ ∴

THE NEXT morning brought the typical hustle of preparing to get back on the road. They ignored Dawnfry, as was normally the case when Johorr felt he needed to get moving quickly. As their bellies rumbled in disagreement, Syl'Kara and Thomlin quickly gathered and stowed Johorr's belongings in their proper place in the carriage.

As Johorr took his seat and snapped the reins to start the horses moving, Syl'Kara and Thomlin kicked dirt over the remnants of the campfire and shuffled up to the back of the carriage as quickly as their shackled legs would allow. Syl'Kara hopped and latched onto its side, placing her feet onto the small bar that hung just behind the rear wheel. It was a position she'd grown accustomed to, and her upper body had grown quite strong over the years from seemingly endless hours perched on the side of a carriage.

Thomlin climbed onto the other side and gave her a wink. He was trying to reassure her that everything was fine, but every time they rode over a bump, rut or rock on the dirt road, his face involuntarily contorted in pain.

Such was the way of things, and she'd known nothing different for longer than she cared to admit. Johorr bought her off of Samuel for a few bottles of whiskey and a bag of silver coins when she was sixty-six years old, and she'd known nothing else ever since.

Her human foster parents, Caden and Geela, eventually died of old age and left her in the care of their daughter Helena. She later married a man named Jacob, and together they continued raising her as if she were part of their family. They, too, died of old age, and passed her along to their only son Samuel.

First, she was a daughter to strange parents, very much unlike herself. She gained a sister in Helena, who eventually became her second mother. Then she gained a brother in Samuel, who she helped to raise and care for, acting as his nanny. When the time came for Samuel to continue her care, as she was still a child and unable to fend for herself, he betrayed her and sold her into slavery for a night of drinking and a few simple coins.

No other elves ever passed through their small village, came to the farm she lived on, or otherwise presented themselves. She was one of a kind, being raised by those with shorter lifespans. While she'd been older than everyone in her family, she was only a child. Even twenty years later, clinging to the side of Johorr's carriage, elven society would not have considered her an adult.

If she forced herself to think about Samuel's actions rationally, she could understand why he sold her to Johorr. They had depleted their land through improper planting techniques and it could barely support enough crops to feed themselves, let alone sell anything to earn enough coin to pay taxes to their Lord. She wasn't of blood relation, even though she was certainly family, by all accounts. When the time came that Samuel's parents had passed and he came face-to-face with the prospect of continuing to care for his slow-to-mature elven sister-nanny—with no end in sight— he understandably took the first chance he could to free himself of the burden. Though she could reason the event in such a way, that hadn't made it hurt any less. His betrayal was real, and she silently wished he would pay dearly for his actions.

She had conversed with one elf in her entire life; a strange fellow named Halidan. He fancied himself a scholar, of sorts, and had paid Johorr for a ride to Tellrindos. They spent many nights talking around the campfire after Johorr drank himself to sleep, whiling away the hours with tales of far-off lands and civilizations that Syl'Kara had never learned about, or even dreamed of. It was from him she learned of the Dynar and Afyr; two very different races of elves with opposing views on life, religion, and the world around them.

The Dynar had black skin, dark hair, and brown eyes. They lived in harmony with the cycle of life, revering death as a necessary contribution to all life that would follow; celebrating the passage of time and the end of days in ways considered obscene by the lofty Afyr. Most of society mistrusted the Dynar, unable to understand their fascination with death, or their motivations for revering it. The worship of Ishnu, goddess of death, was most often viewed as evil by those unfamiliar with the religion. So they lived in isolation, far from human cities and even other elves.

The Afyr had pale skin and silvery, white or golden hair with crystal blue or green eyes. They feared death, and dedicated much of their magical and alchemical research toward prolonging life. Often considered aloof by most outsiders, they valued art, magic, alchemy, and the pursuit of higher knowledge above all else. To most Afyr, the Dynar tendency to welcome, celebrate, and revere death was utterly perverse, and something they could not abide.

'The two standing side by side would seem as if opposite sides of the same coin. The Afyr are as day to the Dynar night,' he'd told her. *'They are not enemies—mind you—they simply do not understand one another, and seem to have no interest in reaching common ground. I, myself, am Ekthri, an elven people of the wood. As a scholar, I have studied all elven cultures to a great extent.*

'You, my dear, are an anomaly. Your skin declares you to be Dynar, while your hair and eyes speak of Afyr blood. I'd wager your mother was an Afyr, for if she were Dynar, you would be in the south—or in the wastelands—living among your people in relative harmony. An Afyr village would have left you to the elements, or at least exiled the woman who birthed you. If I am correct, your mother gave you to a human family to save your life, as well as her own position among her kind.'

Five years had passed since their conversation, and yet his words still rang out in her mind as if he'd just finished speaking them. She had learned more about her people from his brief time accompanying Johorr than she had in her entire life. Johorr had no time for education, nor did he feel it his duty to provide it. They traveled constantly so that he could barter trades that others were unwilling to consider. He trafficked in addictive drugs, poisons, slaves... anything that a reasonable man would detest and avoid.

Everything she knew about her kind had come from one man who joined them for a few short days many winters prior, and that saddened her even more than the routine beatings dished out by her owner; her master; the man she would gladly kill and escape from if she had any idea how to provide for herself afterward. If she'd learned one thing from Johorr, it was that the world was a cruel place and not safe to traverse alone, especially not as a child; certainly not with a socially inept mute under that child's care.

Such thoughts were growing more and more frequent. She was near enough to adulthood to survive in a city, and find a way to make ends meet. More than anything, she yearned to find her own kind. She longed for the company of elves; the company of those who could live as long as she, and experience life on a grander scale. She longed to stop watching those she cared about die all around her.

∴ ∴ ∴

"WHOA!" BELTED Johorr as he pulled back on the reins.

The carriage came to an abrupt and jarring stop in the middle of the road. Syl'Kara had been so distracted by her thoughts that she had seen no indication why they were stopping. The time of day was wrong for one of Johorr's two allowed breaks, and if he were stopping for an extended period of time, he always pulled to the side of the road, if possible.

Dense forest bordered the road to the east and west, and they were at least a full day's ride from the next town. Stopping at such a location could mean only one of two things; a traveler who struck Johorr's interest, or an ambush by bandits. Syl'Kara steeled herself for the worst-case scenario, and quickly hopped down off her perch at the rear of the carriage. Thomlin followed suit and cast her a concerned glance.

"Forgive me, kind sir," came the voice of an old woman standing out of their line of sight. "It has been some time since I have eaten, and I would pay you handsomely for a meal."

"Move out of the way, *hag*, I've no time for beggars!" belted Johorr.

"I've silver for a bite. Surely you've plenty to spare. These *old bones* won't allow me to hunt, and I've quite a journey ahead."

"How much silver ya talkin'?" asked Johorr, his desire for coin evident in his tone.

"A few fiefdom bits for a quick bite, or a handful of Tellrindosian coin for a well-cooked meal and some rations to take with me. If... that's not too much trouble," said the woman.

"Fine. Move out o' the way so I can park up ahead. We'll camp early, and my servants can cook whatever ye fancy," said Johorr.

The old woman chirped her agreement and stepped to the west, coming into view of Syl'Kara. She leaned heavily on a table leg she seemed to use as a cane. Her drab gray robes dragged the ground as she moved, kicking up small puffs of dust with each step. The hunch in her back was very pronounced, as if she hadn't stood properly upright in decades. The skin on her face sagged, as if barely able to cling to her bones for much longer. Without a doubt, she was the oldest creature Syl'Kara had ever witnessed with her own eyes.

Their eyes met briefly as the carriage lurched forward. The woman smiled meekly, as if to say she was thankful for their assistance. To Syl'Kara, there seemed to be something strange beneath her outward appearance. She was sure the old woman was hiding something, but couldn't explain why she felt the way she did about her. An unease crept in, similar to the feeling she had during the strange event the night before.

Thomlin scrambled past her, chasing the rear of the carriage; eager to set about making camp and complete their travels for the day. The chain between his ankles bounced and skittered off the ruts and grooves in the road, breaking her free of the anxiety-riddled thoughts plaguing her mind.

Returning to the moment, Syl'Kara joined Thomlin at the back of the now-parked carriage and began extracting what they would need to camp for the night. She knew the delay would upset Johorr, and he'd likely take it out on the two of them later. However, they'd be safe for the evening, and for that she was thankful to the old woman; Johorr rarely beat them in the presence of strangers.

∴ ∴ ∴

WHEN THEY finished setting camp, Syl'Kara went to work preparing their evening meal. It was far earlier than they normally camped, and she knew that meant they'd be leaving earlier in the morning, likely before the sun entered the sky. Nothing about their circumstances felt right, and she couldn't shake the feeling that something was wrong with the strange woman.

She knelt before the small pit after Thomlin finished placing the fire stones and mindlessly struck her flint and steel together, sending sparks into the kindling therein. The fire roared to life, its flickering flames distracting her for a moment as she tried to break free of the mental funk and anxiety she found herself wallowing in.

Thomlin knelt down and tapped her on the forearm gently, insisting that she hand him the flint and steel. She complied, and he quickly replaced them with an iron pan. As the pan rested atop the logs, flames danced across its underside, slowly warming it enough to cook their meal. Thomlin raced back and forth between the pit and carriage, bringing raw meat, eggs, vegetables and spices to her side so that she could begin her work.

On his last trip to the fire, he brought over a large block of wood, finely shaped, sanded smooth, and routinely treated with oils. He then returned to the carriage and set about preparing drinks for Johorr and their strange guest. Syl'Kara withdrew her cooking knife and started preparing the ingredients atop the traveling butcher's block.

"Who are ye, then?" asked Johorr. "I seen plenty o' travelers, but ne'er an ole woman trav'lin alone in the woods o' the north. So, I figure yer runnin' from sumthin, or ye got no wits about ye. Which is it?"

"I think we're best to leave names out of this. I need food, and you want coin. That's as far as our familiarity need progress," answered the woman.

"Well, I can't jus' call ye 'Woman' all night."

"Call me 'Witch', or 'Hag', if you like. That is what most do. I've no need of names, and no desire to discuss where I've been or where I'm going. I've been through too much, of late, to explain myself to the likes of you," she said. "No offense," she added after having a second thought.

The pan sizzled and hissed as Syl'Kara dropped a hunk of pork trimmings into it off the tip of her knife. Fat rendered slowly into the pan, leaving it greasy and ready to accept her next ingredient. She carefully scooped diced potato and onion into the pan and sprinkled them with salt, dried peppers and blackened garlic. The conversation across from her ceased as the aroma reached them, and their hunger piqued in response.

"Fine. Have it yer way," grumbled Johorr as their ale arrived.

Syl'Kara added two hunks of butter to the pan. As it melted, she slowly spooned the butter over the vegetables, basting them in its creamy goodness.

"Besides, isn't it I that should be curious as to *your* destination in the company of slaves? Not that it's any of my business, but Tellrindos doesn't look kindly on such a practice."

"They know better than ta hassle me. I run trades ta Port Gandraias all the time. The guards know ta look the other way, else they lose their cut o' my payments," he explained.

"Port Gandraias?" she questioned in a very peculiar tone. "You might not find the town as welcoming on this particular trip, I'm afraid."

"Why ye say that?"

The woman seemed to struggle to find the right words, wrinkling her brow in thought. "The city's not quite what it used to be, and they've been beset by tragedy in recent days. I won't go into detail, but suffice to say, there's no trade to be had."

"Bah! Gebrin's expectin' me. Don't matter what befell the place, I got business ta tend. He owes me, and he'll pay what he owes."

"I'm heading south, come morning. Frankly, what you do with your time is your decision-"

"Aye, it is!"

"-but I assure you, it's a waste of time. The town is abandoned."

"Abandoned?" asked Johorr, suddenly perplexed.

"Not a soul in sight," she confirmed.

Syl'Kara calmly nudged the potatoes and onions aside to make room for two steaks, and carefully placed them into the pan. The meat hissed and once again filled the air with an alluring aroma. Thomlin quietly licked his lips in anticipation. He knew she would cook their meal last, but it wasn't often that Johorr let them use their highest quality ingredients. They rarely ate as well as when he had unexpected company and wanted to show off.

"Well, thank ye fer the warnin', but I think I'd rather see that fer myself," said Johorr defiantly.

"You do as you must," sighed the woman.

After the meat spent a few brief minutes on its second side in the pan, Syl'Kara placed one steak and a portion of the potato mixture onto each of the two plates, then returned the pan to the fire. She cracked two eggs into the pan and fried them in more butter while the steaks rested. When the eggs finished cooking, she removed them from the pan and placed one atop each steak.

Thomlin retrieved the plates from Syl'Kara's side and carried them over to Johorr and their guest. The sounds of clanking knives and forks filled the camp as the pair ate their meal in silence, enjoying every bite. Syl'Kara and Thomlin were just beginning their own meals when the pair finished.

"What can you tell me of the lands to the south?" asked the woman as she sat her plate aside.

"What ye after?" asked Johorr, a little put off that the conversation was continuing.

"Have they joined forces to become a kingdom yet?"

"Join forces? Hah!" belted Johorr. "That's 'bout as likely as fire shootin' out my eyes!"

"Any word of an 'Arkhan Vaelin'?" she continued.

"Arkhan who? You sure you ain't out yer wits?"

"I'm just trying to get my bearings. I need to learn what has happened so far, so that I know what is to come."

"How 'bout ye walk down there yerself and find out. I ain't yer scout," he said dismissively. Turning his attention to Thomlin, he added, "fetch me more ale, boy!"

Conversations ceased for the next few hours, while Johorr slowly drank himself to sleep. The woman kept her eyes on Syl'Kara and Thomlin the entire time, studying their activity as they cleaned up from the meal, and prepared the camp for them all to sleep.

∴ ∴ ∴

JOHORR WAS fast asleep several hours before night fell. Thomlin had joined Syl'Kara on the other side of the fire. As soon as Johorr's snores began to ring out, she started tending Thomlin's wounds; dabbing them clean with a damp cloth, and applying fresh ointment.

The old woman watched for a short time, intrigued by the care Syl'Kara showed to her fellow slave. After a few minutes, she got to her feet and crossed the camp to join them. Syl'Kara froze and grew tense, unsure of what to expect. A faint green glow emanated from the woman's outstretched hand as she reached them and cascaded down Thomlin's back. Syl'Kara watched as his skin shimmered and each of the whip marks on his back sealed shut, healing as if they'd never been there.

"Stop! Don't do that!" blurted Syl'Kara.

"Don't you want your friend to be healed?" asked the woman. She released the tension in her hand, and the spell stopped abruptly.

"If these wounds aren't there the next time Johorr whips him, it'll infuriate him further and make him whip even harder," gasped Syl'Kara in fear and frustration. "I know you mean to help, but you've only made things worse!"

"And what if he never whipped you again?" asked the woman as she lowered herself to the ground.

"He will."

"Not if I set you free," said the woman.

"I could set us free myself. We don't need your help with that. There's no point, though. We have nowhere to go once we're free. I'm a half-breed elven child, and he's a mute. Nobody's going to take us in, and we can't earn money on our own. Our lives may be pain, but at least we're alive," explained Syl'Kara sadly.

"Trapped by your situation as much as your shackles, are you?"

"So it would seem, yes," sighed Syl'Kara. "We'll go south eventually, much closer to the Bo'Lari Wastelands. I'll free us then and sneak us south to Haern. Halidan said there's a Dynar village nearby that we could probably find homes in. It's the best we've got, but I can't get us there from here."

"And I am too busy to take you," admitted the old woman.

"Too busy with what?" challenged Syl'Kara, waving her hand to indicate the vast expanse of woods and nothing else around them.

"I must get my bearings so that I can be sure of my next move. I've much to do; far more than I can explain. I just do not know at what time I awoke, and thus what events must follow."

"I don't know what any of that means," admitted Syl'Kara.

"It would be unwise of me to explain, I'm afraid. I know of things to come, but those events will only occur if I am careful and act accordingly."

"So you are a seer?" asked Syl'Kara, a hint of wonder in her tone.

"Not exactly. I haven't seen so much as I've been told, and warned. Suffice to say, that is also how I know you will find no quarter in Port Gandraias, and no trade of any kind either."

"Aye, you said the city was abandoned. I'm afraid Johorr won't listen to you... or me. He has to see things for himself."

"The city isn't so much abandoned as it is deceased. The living never left, though you will not find them there. An unfortunate event has transpired, and I'm afraid that anyone your master might have known there has simply ceased to be."

Syl'Kara felt horrified. The event she witnessed on the horizon, and through the trees, must have happened in Port Gandraias, just as she'd suspected. The energies in the air that night caused a great deal of unease, and she'd been sensing those energies off of the woman in front of her. *That's why I don't trust her! She must have somehow caused whatever happened!*

"Did... did you..." Syl'Kara stammered, unable to voice the question that was burning through her mind. She could tell by the look in the woman's eyes that she understood exactly what her question was, and that the asking displeased her greatly.

"What happened in the port was unfortunate and cannot be undone. That is all you need to know."

Syl'Kara's mind suddenly filled with tales of an ancient witch that wandered the lands. A witch that was said to move through shadows and have control over darkness; a powerful being feared by the gods themselves. She once thought the tales to be nonsense; terrible stories meant to shock the listener, or scare children into doing as they were told. The realization struck that the tales might be true; that the woman before her might be that very witch.

Her horror slowly became evident as her eyes grew wide. Thomlin looked back at her as the conversation suddenly ceased and started to panic. He turned himself around and grabbed Syl'Kara by the shoulders, attempting to shake her free of whatever spell she was under.

"I mean you no harm, young one," said the old woman reassuringly. "All I sought was a meal, and that you have provided."

"You... you're... but you..." stammered Syl'Kara.

"I am who you fear I am, but the tales are far from accurate... I assure you. I do not run around eating children for disobeying their parents, nor do I kill for sport or entertainment. Neither do I *drink souls*, or whatever other nonsense is floating around about me. I simply do as I must, when I must," she said dismissively.

Thomlin looked at Syl'Kara, confused and afraid.

"Will you tell me of the lands to the south? I fear my memory has been scrambled and I am still coming to grips with my new reality. I cannot tell if what I remember has come to pass, or is still destined," asked the woman.

"I... I fear I do not know much of value," said Syl'Kara, her voice quivering. She patted Thomlin's shoulder reassuringly, and tried her best to hide the fear on her face for his benefit.

"Have there been talks of unification?"

"None of the street folk in Uldenheim or the other northern villages have mentioned anything of the sort. They... they all seem in fear of attack from other fiefdoms, or from the Toor. There was talk of Uldenheim raiding the Afyr for weaponry, since they refused assistance, but we didn't stay long enough to see if that actually happened," explained Syl'Kara.

"Then I am not too late," said the old woman, nodding. "I think I know when I am, and what I must do."

"Where will you go?"

"I am not headed as far south as you might wish, if that is why you are asking. My destination is for me to know," she answered. Puzzled, she leaned forward and looked Syl'Kara in the eyes. "Are you suggesting that, even though I am the Night Witch that you fear—the Nightweaver—that you would travel with me, were I to agree to take you south? Despite your fears that I would harm you?" she asked.

"Is that so surprising?" answered Syl'Kara. "I... do fear you; that much is true. You healed Thomlin, and I am guessing you could have easily killed us and taken your food without the hassle of bartering with Johorr... but you didn't. It is most likely as you say; the tales are not accurate. So, yes, were you traveling south toward

Haern I would gladly accompany you to freedom, and leave Johorr behind. I would have to take Thomlin, though, and his presence would burden you."

"There are two things that you can trust. The first is that if I meant you harm, this conversation would not be happening. You are, therefore, safe in my presence. The second is that I am not fit to provide care for an elven child and her mute companion. I simply lack the patience, and the time, to look after *anyone* properly, and my path would only put you in harm's way.

"If this were any other time, I would have taken you to Haern myself. That said, I think you are braver than you give yourself credit for. It may not happen today, or even tomorrow, but sometime soon you will find the rest of the courage you need to take your stand and gain your freedom. Of that I have confidence. When that happens, you will find your way to Haern without any need for assistance.

"I also believe that we will meet again, in due time. To ensure that we do, I present you with this," she said, presenting a small piece of hematite for Syl'Kara to take. "It is nothing of note, and will inspire neither jealousy nor greed from Johorr should he find it upon your person. A simple stone you could have found on your travels, and nothing more to the untrained eye. Keep it with you. Someday, it will guide you to me, so that I might know you are safe and have become the woman I see within you.

"Or, toss it away and be comforted in the knowledge that our paths might never cross again. The choice is yours, though I do hope you choose the former. I will eventually need help to bring my plans to fruition, and I have a feeling you could be vital to my efforts. Despite what the world might think of me, I am not the one who should be feared. I seek only to prepare the world for what comes next; that which deserves all our fear... even mine. Some day, we will all fight that common foe, whether we choose to or not.

"Until that time," she continued as she gained her feet, "I leave you in peace, and with a shield of protection for the night to come, so that you might contemplate in safety upon the words I have spoken," she finished. With a twitch of her finger, a powerful burst of energy washed over the camp and encircled them in a shimmering, translucent black dome. "Stay inside the camp and you will be protected until dawn. No harm shall come to you, and Johorr will not wake."

Syl'Kara looked down at the small stone in her palm, and then back toward the woman, but she had vanished. No sign of her remained, and no footprints led away from where she'd been standing. It was simply as if she'd never been there in the first place.

Thomlin gasped and whipped his head from left to right, trying to find the strange woman. Syl'Kara tried her best to calm him. After a few hours of reassurance, he was fast asleep, and Syl'Kara returned to the fire to reflect on what had transpired.

DETRITUS

Ris'Nammlil, Amaethur 14th, 575 of the 1st Era

THE NEXT day progressed as most did in the company of Johorr. He didn't speak of the strange woman they'd met the night before, and seemed to question the small pouch of silver he found on his lap when he awoke in the morning.

Thomlin similarly behaved as if nothing had happened. He even presented his back to Syl'Kara for her to reapply the healing ointment to his wounds during their mid-day break, as if he'd completely forgotten that Nightweaver healed him.

Why am I the only one that remembers? Is it the stone she gave me? Did she do something to them? Was it the spell she placed upon the camp?

The questions burned in Syl'Kara's mind all day during their travels. She was so lost in thought, at several points she almost fell from her perch at the rear of the carriage; oblivious to the fact that they'd entered a patch of bumpy terrain. Normally, she'd have noticed well in advance and adjusted her grip on the side of the carriage accordingly.

Before she knew it, their day of travel had ended, and they were rounding the bend on the final stretch of road before entering Port

Gandraias. She recognized the south entrance to the city, having passed through it countless times during her years of servitude.

The decrepit, rotting wooden sign still stood precariously over the road. A sign she was sure should have fallen many years prior to their arrival. If she was a gambler, she'd have wagered with Thomlin or even Johorr after their last visit that the sign wouldn't be there the next time they returned. There it stood, just to spite her.

Small patches of cobble dotted the otherwise haphazard dirt road, adding to the treacherous nature of its use rather than aiding. Deep ruts cut into the dirt and clay, leading toward bits of stone paving that then jolted the carriage upright before descending again into the carved path on the other side. Over and over, the carriage heaved and dropped onto and off of the remnants of a once prominent and well-maintained road. Long gone were the days of its construction, and so to the care of those responsible for its upkeep.

Bushes, weeds and vines crept onto, around, and over the road; creating arches and canopies of life that seemed to hint that one was entering a garden rather than Tellrindos's primary trade port. The city came into view beyond, standing in stark contrast to the natural beauty of the plants and trees that surrounded it on three sides.

Many of the buildings in the southern sections of the city were boarded up, indeed abandoned, as Nightweaver had stated; not that Johorr remembered her warning. Down the western road, several buildings seemed to have recently exploded, for lack of a better explanation. Syl'Kara imagined the devastation to be quite similar to what would happen if someone were to fire cannons at the city for days on end. Bits of debris lay strewn across the entire southwestern district, and several buildings were missing entirely; as was the inn Johorr favored; their usual first stop upon arrival.

Johorr stopped the carriage and climbed down, surprise written all over his face. Thomlin hopped down and followed Johorr dutifully as he began searching the debris for clues as to what might have happened. Syl'Kara calmly stepped down from her perch and studied the view before her.

Somehow, that burst of light and the strange noises I heard must have been what caused the destruction, but where is everyone?

She thought back to what Nightweaver had said about the town. *'The living never left, though you will not find them there.'* With that thought in mind, she looked harder for signs of life, or death. Any sign that might reveal what had happened to the people who lived in Port Gandraias.

Johorr and Thomlin headed straight for the pile of debris where the inn had once stood. Syl'Kara turned right, facing east down the road in front of it. Wisps of ash drifted into the air on the breeze, barely visible in the failing light of day, rising up from small piles dotting the ground in every direction.

She knelt down next to a pile and studied it with her right hand while thumbing the small piece of hematite on her left. Most of the ash had piled into an oval pattern, with two thin lines leading away from the center mass. At the end of one line of ash, a bit of gold caught the light and glimmered as if calling out to her. She poked the bit of gold, and it clanked to the ground and rolled. An unadorned gold ring came to a rest near her foot.

A small, quick yelp involuntarily escaped her lips as she shot upright. Her hands instinctively went to her face to cover her mouth and stifle any further outbursts. She didn't know why she felt the need to keep quiet, but she was certain succumbing to the panic that was growing inside her would only lead to places she didn't want to go; both mentally and physically. She had to keep herself together, and that meant forcing herself to remain as calm as she could.

"What is it?" asked Johorr. His voice had a hint of what she could've mistaken for concern. Under the circumstances, she expected his response might have been reasonable. His tone struck her as odd, however, since he had shown no concern for her wellbeing at all up to that point.

"They're people," answered Syl'Kara, just above a whisper. She pointed at several piles around them as she continued, "those piles; all of them. They are people turned to ash. The breeze is picking them up. We're... breathing them!" She covered her mouth and nose with her sleeve, horrified. Thomlin followed suit and tried to wipe the taste out of his mouth for good measure.

"No, that ain't it. Can't be," protested Johorr. She pointed at the ring next to her foot. He knelt, picked it up and studied it for a time, then looked her in the eyes. "Where'd you find this?"

"It rolled out of that pile of ash... at the end of that line... where the person's hand used to be," she explained meekly. She backed away a few steps, accidentally stepping into another pile, and squealed faintly again, realizing what she'd done.

"What in tha hells happened 'ere? This is Gebrin's ring! If he's dead, we wasted the whole fuckin' trip!" Johorr kicked the ash.

The remnants of a pair of leather boots went skittering across the ground. The golden emblem on the heels signified they were Gebrin's. "He's sposed ta pay in *gold* this trip! Ten bags o' opium, wasted! Three weeks o' travel with ye sorry lot, wasted! Gods damn it!"

Thomlin ducked to the ground and cowered as Johorr stormed past him, fearful that his master would take the situation out on the two of them. Johorr reached the remnants of his favorite inn and started throwing pieces off the pile in anger.

"It's gotta be 'ere somewhere. Help me dig, ya good-fer-nuthins!"

"But-" started Syl'Kara.

"If this gold ring survived, his bag o' gold did too. Get diggin'!"

∴ ∴ ∴

NIGHT FELL before they found anything of any significance. Johorr had become wrathful and resorted to stomping around in a huff, kicking piles of ash and cursing under his breath at his '*luck*'. Syl'Kara and Thomlin both had bloody knuckles and several splinters, but nothing else to show for their efforts.

"Should... we make camp?" asked Syl'Kara sheepishly, nervous that her question would turn Johorr's anger toward herself.

"Fine!" spouted Johorr. He stomped toward the carriage, grabbed the reins, and led the carriage down the main road to the south, to the other side of the few surviving buildings in the district.

They got to their feet to follow, but before they took a step, the pile of rubble behind them shifted. Syl'Kara grabbed at Thomlin's arm to move him away from the impending avalanche, but he resisted. He held up one finger, indicating that she should give him a minute. He'd seen something; something she hadn't.

The debris lifted slightly, as if something underneath was trying to push its way through. Thomlin knelt back down and started moving chunks of wood and stucco out of the way. Syl'Kara looked on, intrigued by the turn of events but concerned for what it meant.

After a few minutes, a hand appeared from below the pile. The hand was pale, and the arm attached to it was shrouded in several layers of translucent, black silk; silk that should have been shredded by the debris the hand was reaching through, but somehow seemed completely intact. The hand, in fact, showed no signs of injury. Both details raised Syl'Kara's suspicions, and made her uneasy. She felt the same unnatural energy as she had during the event a few nights before, and once again in the presence of Nightweaver.

I don't like this!

Thomlin continued removing the debris that was blocking the person beneath from climbing free of the pile. A small door eventually pushed its way out of the floor, casting the remaining rubble aside and revealing a cellar beneath the building. Thomlin reached down and lent his hands to the person trapped within, lifting them free of the cellar and helping them down the pile to safety.

The same black silk adorned the figure from neck to ankle. Layer upon layer of silk, shifting in the breeze; each translucent and giving a shimmering effect that made it nearly impossible to see their true form. The only parts of them that were exposed were their hands and feet, both with small bits of silk stretching over top, looping around a few fingers and toes to keep the outfit in place.

Jet black hair flowed down its back and perfectly framed its white mask; which appeared to be carved from a single, massive pearl. Formless and featureless, it gave the vague impression that a person's face was somewhere underneath, and yet offered no obvious way for that person to see, speak, or breathe.

Thomlin seemed immediately smitten; completely struck by the unnatural beauty of the person before him. He couldn't speak to say as much, but Syl'Kara could clearly see the look in his eyes. She, too, found herself inexplicably aroused by the person's presence. Such arousal was not normal for an elven girl at her age, and the sudden emergence of those feelings furthered her unease.

The creature bowed at the hip, bent slightly at the knees, and fanned their hands out to the side, as if stuck somewhere between a formal bow and a curtsy. *Perhaps it is meant to be nondescript,* wondered Syl'Kara. The thing's pearl mask whipped around instantly to *gaze* upon her, as if it had heard her thoughts. Syl'Kara jumped back a step involuntarily, a cold wave of fear washing over her.

Johorr stormed back around the corner of the building he'd disappeared behind, spouting profanities under his breath at the uselessness of his servants. "What did ye find, boy?" he belted, half curious and half dismissive.

Thomlin stepped out of the way to let him see the creature completely. Johorr stopped briefly in his tracks, taken aback by the mysterious thing before him. The moons Provoss and Aygos provided just enough light for him to see the being, and he seemed instantly intrigued.

He walked toward their new arrival, his right hand outstretched. It walked lithely toward him, and met him halfway. He bent down to meet the pearl mask at eye level, and it reached up, gently stroking his cheek with its right hand. After a moment, he sighed, blinked twice as if clearing his vision, and stood upright. He put out his left hand for the creature to take, and yelled to them, "She's coming with us. We can't leave her to whatever fate befell this town."

The clarity of his speech and the change in his demeanor immediately struck Syl'Kara as odd. Something was amiss, and *she*, whoever *she was*, was somehow behind it.

∴ ∴ ∴

JOHORR KICKED down the door in front of their parked carriage. The former residents had boarded its doors and windows months, or years, prior, and its empty interior echoed wildly at the sound of his entry. He carefully escorted the silk-clad woman into the old home as if she were his prized possession. Once she was inside, he then turned to Syl'Kara and said, "I want you to cook the finest meal you've ever prepared. Our guest deserves nothing less than perfection."

"Why are you–"

"Do not question me. Siscci is our honored guest, and we are privileged to be in her presence. Do as I tell you," he demanded.

"How do you know her name? She hasn't spoken."

"She speaks. You are simply unworthy of hearing," he answered. "Don't fret, that will change in time. She has come for the benefit of all. Give it time, and you will see for yourself. Now... do as I command."

Syl'Kara exited the building and returned to the carriage, confused and more than a little frightened. Thomlin joined her and eagerly began gathering ingredients for their meal. She placed a hand atop his as he reached for a small sack of fresh vegetables.

"Did you hear her speak?" she asked.

Thomlin nodded vigorously, with excitement in his eyes. He turned to continue his task, but she interrupted again.

"Why doesn't this frighten you?"

He pulled his hand free of her touch, scowled as if offended by her question, and resumed his task. She never wanted him to have the power of speech more in her life than she did at that moment. Nothing about their situation felt right to her.

.˙. .˙. .˙.

SYL'KARA PREPARED their meal alone in the home's kitchen. She spent an hour cleaning the room enough to be of use, and another hour cleaning the stovepipe so that she didn't fill the home with smoke while cooking. Even with the delays, neither Thomlin nor Johorr came to find out what was taking so long, or offer any assistance. In Thomlin's case, the lack of his help was completely out of character.

She prepared four plates, and made two trips to the room in which they'd gathered. After she placed the last plate in front of Siscci, the pearl mask simply nodded in thanks and nothing more.

They ate in complete silence. Neither Johorr nor Thomlin took their eyes off of Siscci. Syl'Kara wasn't even sure they knew what she'd served them. Siscci sat quietly for the entire meal, switching her gaze between the two men and otherwise never moving. She made no attempt to lift or remove her mask to eat; the meal, it seemed, was inconsequential to her.

Syl'Kara quietly gathered their wooden plates once the three of them had finished, and cleaned everything used during the cooking and dining process. Neither of the men said a word as she went back to work. An hour later, when she returned to the chamber to see if Johorr needed anything else for the evening, Thomlin and Siscci were no longer present.

"Where's Thomlin?" she asked with hesitation, unsure if Johorr would lash out for questioning him.

"He is receiving her gift," he answered with a smile.

"Her gift?" she asked, perplexed. Everything felt wrong. The woman, their behavior, the state of the town, meeting Nightweaver the night before, the strange event the night before that... *what is happening*, she wondered in a panic.

"Siscci has a gift for us all. You will have your turn. For now, sleep. We're heading north in the morning," he explained. There was an air to his voice that seemed wholly unnatural. He was speaking, and she could see him, but it was as if he was somewhere else entirely.

"North? But we never venture north of Port Gandraias. You said we-"

"We are heading to Helmdale. That is the nearest town, and where Siscci wants to be, so that is where we will go. We can't let her travel alone," his voice grew ever-so-slightly angrier as he spoke, warning her not to push the issue.

She moved to the far side of the room, leaned back into a corner, and slid to the floor, tucking her knees near her chest. It wasn't long before her exhaustion set in, and the unusually deep sleep of a growing elf took over. She resisted as long as she could, waiting to see if Thomlin would return, but he still hadn't by the time she finally succumbed. She never once saw Johorr move from his spot, drink any of his ale, or take his eyes off the door through which Thomlin and Siscci must have departed.

∴ ∴ ∴

THE NEXT morning, she awakened to the sound of the rest of the group moving about the room. Thomlin was busy packing the few things they'd brought in from the carriage, while Johorr followed a pacing Siscci around like he was her pet.

"Oh, you're awake!" chirped Thomlin with a smile.

Syl'Kara's breath caught in her throat. *Thomlin can't speak! How is he speaking? What is happening?*

Siscci stopped in her tracks, her face whipping around toward Syl'Kara in an instant. She slowly turned and faced Thomlin, then tilted her head ever so slightly to one side. Thomlin's face seemed to drain of blood, as if he'd been caught doing something he shouldn't. After a few seconds, his complexion returned to normal, then he simply nodded to Syl'Kara and walked outside with the bedroll draped over his arm.

Syl'Kara sat for a moment and tried to fight off the sense of dread that grew within her. Siscci nearly glided across the room, her delicate feet seeming to hover above the floor as she passed. She stopped in front of Syl'Kara and bent at the hip, lowering her mask down to Syl'Kara's eye level. Her head tilted to one side and then the other before leaning in closer, nearly coming into contact with Syl'Kara's forehead.

The hiss of rushing air escaped around the edges of her mask as she stood upright abruptly—clearly frustrated—then turned and left the room.

Johorr walked over in Siscci's wake and extended a hand to the elven girl. "Come. We are leaving," he said plainly, his eyes still fixed upon their guest.

Unsure of what was going on, and fearing that she was already treading on thin ice with the strange woman, Syl'Kara took Johorr's hand and let him lift her to her feet. Nothing about that simple gesture was normal. Johorr didn't offer assistance. Ever.

Syl'Kara tried her best to stifle her thoughts while she followed them outside. Everything was wrong. Ever since they arrived in Port Gandraias, the world seemed to be in a state of upheaval. She slowed her pace to gather her thoughts, hoping that distance would allow her to think clearly without Siscci listening in.

Thomlin can speak, where he previously couldn't. He also hasn't acted himself since he pulled Siscci from the pile of debris. Johorr is acting as if he's Siscci's servant, rather than our master. Neither of them are behaving like themselves.

Every living creature in town was rendered unto dust, using the same energies I sensed emanating from Nightweaver. I think she's the one who did it. If I'm right, then this Siscci either wasn't here when it happened, or somehow survived it when nobody else could. If I'm wrong, then Siscci caused it. In either case, we're in danger as long as she's around. Or... is it just me that's in danger because she can't control me?

Why can't she control me?

PRELUDE

THE RIDE to Helmdale was pure and utter torment for Syl'Kara. Thomlin and Siscci sat on the bench at the front of the carriage with Johorr; a seat he rarely shared. She clung to her perch at the back, as always, trying to hide her thoughts the entire trip; a task that proved nearly impossible. The effort made her day seem to last forever, and that was exacerbated by the fact that Johorr never once stopped to take a break. By late afternoon, Syl'Kara had lost the battle with her bladder, and had unwillingly relieved herself while still hanging off the back of the carriage.

When they finally reached the village, her fingers had almost given out. She'd been holding onto the outside of the carriage for the last few hours by draping her right arm over the lip. Her bicep was purple from bruising; beaten and battered by every bump in the road during the last leg of the trip. They finally came to a stop in front of a small inn in the center of town just before nightfall.

She slid to the ground, shaking from fatigue and smelling faintly of urine. They hadn't eaten or taken any time to rest. She wasn't sure how their horses had managed to pull the carriage for an entire day, or how any of the passengers on the bench had made it the whole way without relieving themselves. *I'd trade that ride for one of Johorr's beatings any day*, she thought with a sigh.

Johorr and Thomlin climbed down from the carriage and each raised their hands to help Siscci. She presented an arm to each of them and allowed them to lift and lower her to the ground. Syl'Kara slumped to the ground—unable to convince her legs to keep her upright any longer—and watched as they escorted the silken woman through the doors of the inn.

A few minutes later, a middle-aged, heavyset woman came and helped her to her feet. "You poor thing. Let me get you a meal... and a bath," she offered sympathetically.

"Thank you," said Syl'Kara, her voice revealing her apprehension.

"Oh, it's no trouble," said the woman as she wrapped an arm around Syl'Kara and started walking her inside. "I'll see you're treated proper. Anyone fit to travel with Siscci deserves nothing less."

"Do... you know who she is?" asked Syl'Kara, uncertain what version of this strange woman she was interacting with. *Is this really her, or has she too been changed by Siscci?*

"Don't be silly, deary. Deep down, we all know who she is."

I don't, thought Syl'Kara. *I'm not sure I want to.*

The interior of the inn was much darker than Syl'Kara expected. The only source of light came from the few feeble rays of sunset coming in through the windows. A human woman barely taller than Syl'Kara was hurrying around the room, trying to prepare for the coming night's patrons; placing candles and small baskets of bread on each table. The room smelled of stale hops, rendering lard and boiled cabbage; a combination that normally wouldn't have affected her overly much, but she hadn't been feeling well before she entered.

She quickly pushed herself free of the woman's grasp, barged back through the swinging doors and out into the street. Her stomach tried its best to empty its contents, but she hadn't eaten since the night before. The woman that'd been helping her returned to her side and used a handkerchief to dab away the few specs of stomach acid that lined her lips; little else had come up in her heaves.

"Can... can I dine outside? I don't want to be any trouble," said Syl'Kara, still on her hands and knees in the dirt. *Plus it will keep me away from her*, she thought.

"Certainly, my dear. There's a small patio in the rear used by the servers when they go on break. You can dine there."

"Do you really get so many patrons? The town looks fairly small, but the inn seems equipped to handle far more people."

"We do okay, I reckon. Folk come down from Belaigne most nights—usually the same folk—and we get travelers all the time, heading one way or another along the queen's road. Rare is the night we aren't full, and with you lot in town, I expect we'll have more than we can handle," answered the woman excitedly. "Name's Bess. I own the place. I'll see to it you're treated very well tonight. After all, you brought her to us."

Syl'Kara grunted in discomfort, both mental and physical, while Bess helped her to her feet and toward the side of the building. Once they'd reached the patio, the owner led her to a post to lean on while she pulled the chairs down off of the exterior table and got everything ready. It wasn't long before Bess was back at her side, helping her to her seat.

"Thank you, Bess. You are too kind to a poor slave like me."

"Oh bother. Where are my manners? She said I could remove those from you, and Sire Johorr even handed me the key," she said as she rummaged in her skirt pocket. Bess didn't notice the shock on Syl'Kara's face when she knelt to undo the shackles. She left a few moments later after giving one last reassuring smile.

A short while later, the diminutive serving girl came out with a basket of bread, a steaming bowl of stew, a plate of baked beans in a creamy white sauce, and a mug of ale. She placed the meal on the table and left with nothing more than a smile. It was the best meal Syl'Kara had eaten in a very long time; mostly because she hadn't cooked it herself, and she wouldn't have to wash the dishes afterward. Syl'Kara was quite unaccustomed to being served, and her ankles were eerily cold without her shackles.

∴ ∴ ∴

THE MEAL was everything she'd needed it to be; warm, filling, and full of nourishment, even if it was a tad bland for her liking. Humans always seemed rushed, in her eyes; ever willing to sacrifice quality for the sake of speed. She couldn't know for certain that elves lived any differently, but her dramatically slow physical progression and tendency to fall into flights of fancy, rather than focus on a particular task for too long, hadn't come from her foster parents. She could only assume that she represented what most elves must be, and that told her they must certainly take their time to do things properly, rather than focusing on how fast they could get things done.

Studying the meal had been a welcome reprieve from her thoughts of late. Her entire life—as pathetic and hopeless as it might have been—had crumbled around her in recent days, and she feared that whatever was happening was only the beginning. She'd outlived several generations of her foster family, and spent the equivalent of an average human's *good* adult years as a slave to a despicable man. Her circumstances had deprived her of eighty-six years of learning and exploration.

How much of the world could she have seen, had she lived a normal life? What could the elders of an elven community have taught her? Could she have learned something—during that life she never had a chance to live—that would have prepared her for the events unfolding around her?

I can't think like that, she lamented. *I still don't understand what's going on. Who is this Siscci, and what is she doing to people? And how? How did she survive Port Gandraias, and how is she changing people into something... new?*

She pushed the dishes away from herself and shifted her chair. Her strength was returning, and that was promising. *I might have to run. If she starts reading my mind now, I'm probably done for. I hope she's far enough away. Even if she isn't, I have to work this out. I have to think this through.*

In her new position, she could see through the back door, the kitchen door, and out into the bar itself. She sat and watched for what felt like hours as patrons seemed to pour in, filling the room to the point that they began to stand in clusters between tables and perch on the stairs.

Where did they all come from, and why come here? Is it her? Has her influence reached so far already?

The crowd started splitting down the middle. She couldn't see why, but had her suspicions. Slowly, she got out of her chair and crept through the kitchen's open doors, closer to the crowd beyond. Siscci was descending the stairs, headed for the main floor. She could only see the hint of the mysterious woman's silk garb just past the steps and railing, but that was enough to know for certain. The crowd was making way for her to join them, and a very loud and elated Johorr seemed to follow in her wake.

She must have taken him upstairs, like she took Thomlin off in secret last night. Is she doing what I think she's doing? Has he been up there with her since we arrived?

"Siscci is here to choose. Only one will ascend and experience the wonders that I have borne witness to. Be not afraid, for all will have their turn!" announced Johorr. He stood at the lower landing of the stairs, looming over the crowd as if he were running a brothel, and Siscci was his only employee.

Yes, that must be what's happening, at least at the basest level. No woman holds such sway over so many, no matter who she is. They can't even see what she looks like! There must be more to it. It can't just be sex.

Men and women swooned across the crowd whenever she drew near. Her silk outfit drifted in and out of view as she walked amongst the throng, her hand lighting upon the cheek of each person, one after another. Eventually, she stopped at a mountain of a man, far larger and stronger than anyone else in the establishment. She grabbed his hand gently and tugged toward the stairs. If it weren't for her garb, Syl'Kara would have described the way she moved and interacted as sultry, in every sense of the word she could imagine. It seemed as if she left nothing to chance; every movement was a calculated attempt at manipulation.

As she led the man away, the room was deathly silent. When the pair finally went out of view on the stairs, a woman in the middle of the crowd remarked, "I've never been attracted to a woman before. She's so beautiful."

"I've never seen such a striking brunette... and her eyes, they-" started a man, but he was quickly interrupted.

"Brunette? She clearly has red hair. Those flowing locks are unmistakable. How could you not s-" started another.

"You're both daft! She's a blond Afyr; the rarest of their kind!" insisted a third man.

"Enough!" belted Johorr. "She is whatever you most desire! She has come to fulfill your needs, and bring harmony to your lives; peace like you've never known before. She can be whatever you wish her to be. Think about that while you wait. She will select another lucky soul on the morrow."

An icy chill ran down Syl'Kara's spine. *What kind of spell caster can do such a thing? Is she an illusionist? An enchantress? Why would she do this? What's her end game?*

She shook the thoughts from her head and forced herself to focus. *I need to see what she's really doing with the people she takes. If it's just sex, fine. I'll go find someone to counter her spells... if I can. If it's something else—something worse—I may just have to run for my life, and hope she doesn't find me.*

∴ ∴ ∴

AFTER A quick look around to get her bearings, she backed out of the kitchen into the chill night air. Her bare feet weren't as phased by colder climes as a human's would be, but she found herself wishing she owned a pair of boots. Once she was outside, in relative safety, she studied the back of the building, looking for a way to ascend. She knew the stairs were far too crowded for her to slip by; impossible if Johorr was still standing guard.

One of the rooms on the second floor had a private balcony. She presumed it might be the most expensive suite in the inn, facing the scenery at the rear of the building, rather than the busy, dirty street to the front. There were several pipes exiting the wall by her side, used to exhaust the smoke from stoves in the kitchen. Above them was a sign indicating that the rear entrance was only for staff, and just over that was a small ledge that wrapped around the building, acting as a barrier between the lower and upper floor.

She studied her possible route for a moment, and then went into action. There hadn't been a lot of opportunities to climb in the past few decades—let alone scale a building—but she had fond memories of climbing trees with Samuel when he was still a child. He'd often commented on just how nimble she was, and how it was so unfair that he couldn't climb as quickly or as easily as she. *I guess it's time to put that to the test,* she mused.

Reaching the first set of pipes on her own was nigh impossible. They were located most of the way up the wall of the first floor, and she was still just under five feet tall. She grabbed her chair, being careful to not let it bang the table or scrape against the cobblestone patio, and carried it over to the wall. She sat it down carefully with its back against the wall and deftly hopped onto the seat and then the edge of its back.

Balancing on her tiptoes, she reached for the first pipe and found purchase, then immediately withdrew her hands and blew on them gently. Unsurprisingly, the pipe was scalding hot. *Well, I guess they are cooking,* she scolded herself.

Syl'Kara drew the small cooking knife Johorr let her keep on her hip and cut off a few scraps of her brown, threadbare tunic. She folded the strips into multiple layers, wrapped one around each hand, and tied them into place with help from her teeth. After returning the small knife to its sheath, she readied herself and tried the pipe again. It was warm, and the protection wouldn't last for long, but she felt she could get by. Before proceeding, though, she hopped down and prepared similar coverings for her feet.

When she was finally ready, she returned to the chair, grabbed the first pipe and slowly raised herself until she was standing on top of it. The pipe wasn't far from the wall, and she nearly fell twice getting to her feet.

She grabbed the next highest pipe, which was further from the wall, and lifted herself until the pipe rested against her waist, then slowly raised up onto one knee, and then the arches of her feet. She was sure the process had given her a few mild burns, but there was no other way up, and she needed to see for herself what was going on.

Balancing precariously on the single pipe, she reached for the sign. *Crap*, she thought angrily. The top edge was just out of reach. Resigning herself to receive more burns, she stepped onto the balls of her feet, squatted down and leaped upward, sending her just high enough to find purchase. She gripped the sign with all her strength, latching on similarly to how she'd held onto the carriage when she first began her travels with Johorr.

Crossing one hand over another, she moved closer to the balcony, then raised her feet as she'd done before, putting her feet almost at hip level. With all her strength, she jumped upward, searching for the ledge that would take her the rest of the way. She nearly missed.

Her momentum carried her slightly away from the wall, putting the ledge dangerously far from her center mass. She barely caught the edge with the tips of her fingers, and grunted involuntarily as her body weight abruptly pulled downward, nearly ripping them loose and sending her plummeting.

With great effort, she carefully shifted her grip until more of her fingers were in contact with the upper edge of the small, thin ledge, then worked her way toward the balcony. Once there, she reached up and out with her left hand and grabbed onto the floor of the balcony, just under the railing. A few moments later, she was up and over the railing, her feet firmly planted, and in no danger of falling.

Syl'Kara took a moment to calm her racing heart before getting any nearer to the window. She was instantly thankful that she'd come over the railing at the door, and that the door was made from solid wood. There was no way she'd have been able to hide her presence as she flopped over and onto the balcony, panting and gasping from the effort, in full view of a window.

∴ ∴ ∴

THE WINDOW looked in on a room that was lit by a wooden chandelier holding three candles. It was higher quality lighting than any inn she'd ever seen in her life, but far simpler than the artistic, golden chandeliers she'd heard tales of from other travelers.

A single bed sat on the right side of the room, just on the other side of the door. An armoire was up against the far wall, with a small table and chair on either side of it. From what she could tell, the room was fairly high quality for such a small town, and certainly better than any she'd ever stayed in.

The large man from downstairs was standing at the foot of the bed, his clothes crumpled in a pile on the floor nearby. Siscci was slowly standing up in front of him, running her hands along his sides and up onto his chest; her body still fully covered in silk, and her mask still on. That didn't seem to have deterred the man's interests in the slightest.

She reached both hands for the man's neck, and he bent down to make it easier for her to reach. The pair met in what would have been a kiss, had his lips met her own. After a few brief moments, she backed away from him, but he did not move. He stayed in position, his lips pursed as if still connecting with her. His eyes were closed, and he seemed to have stopped breathing.

Siscci took a full step back and slowly reached her hand toward her mask. Syl'Kara's heart raced again, not from physical effort but in anticipation of what might be underneath. She was instantly happy that the strange woman was so preoccupied with her quarry, and not paying attention to any thoughts that might be echoing out on her balcony.

A faint hiss escaped Siscci as the mask pulled away. Streams of mucus and blobs of puss streamed between the mask and her proper face, snapping when extended too far and dripping to the floor with little plops. The face underneath was putrid and covered in a thin layer of black slime. Her skin was leathery and grew scaly the further it was from her face.

There was no nose to speak of, just a small bump and two slanted slits where one should have been. Her mouth opened slowly, but instead of a single opening there were several vertical slits, as if her skin had sealed together at several places across her lips. It stretched as she opened her mouth, looking like a soft, fleshy cage guarding her mouth. Her eyes were pitch black, with three small, red, vertical lines where her irises should have been, and when she blinked, her lids closed vertically.

Syl'Kara's heart stopped for a moment. The sheer terror of what she was seeing completely overcame her. She had no words for what Siscci's true form was, aside from the knowledge that she wasn't any of the sentient, goodly races or even monsters she'd ever heard tales of. A scream attempted to escape her lips, but all that came out was a faint click as a tiny burst of air popped through the gap between the back of her tongue and the roof of her mouth.

Siscci took a step forward and placed her strange mouth up against the man's pursed lips. She sucked with all her might. As she slowly leaned back, green energies streamed out of the man's mouth and into her own.

The man's skin began to gray and wrinkle. His hair slowly turned white, and his cheeks sunk into his face. He dried up and decayed before Syl'Kara's eyes, and all she could do was watch in horror; frozen in place by her own inability to overcome her fear. After seconds that felt like an eternity, his body fell to the ground. The sound of its fall reminded her of dropping kindling next to a campfire atop a pile of dry leaves. She could taste bile in the back of her throat, and forced herself to swallow it back. Just as she was about to turn and escape the balcony, Siscci moved forward.

With a series of hisses, snarls and growls, Siscci chanted a spell. A shadowy, crimson form separated from her body, coalesced atop the man's crumpled corpse and slowly melded into him. Her incantation complete, she placed the pearl mask back on her face and moved toward the bed to lie down.

The man's skin moistened and regained its color. His hair returned to its natural state, if not cleaner and shinier than before. Air rushed past his lips with a faint whistle, and his chest heaved with the intake of air. His muscles twitched, and his body straightened into a more natural position on the floor. After a few moments, he blinked and sat upright. He looked over at Siscci as she rested on the bed, then nodded once at her saying, "As you wish."

Syl'Kara didn't stick around to find out what Siscci wished. She figured she had the time it took for the man to get dressed before they discovered her, and that it was best to use the time she had to get back to the ground and leave town.

Unsure how long she had, and more than a little panicked after what she'd just witnessed, she sat on the railing, swung her legs over and dropped down without hesitation. She rolled as she landed, in an attempt to reduce her chance for injuries, but still managed to twist her left ankle in the process.

It was late fall, and the ground was only slightly warmer than the cool night air. She was wearing less clothing than when the night began, her feet were bare, her ankle was twisted, and she was fairly sure she'd just witnessed a demon drink a man's soul. None of that was going to stop her from getting out of that town as fast as she possibly could.

AMELIORATION

Ris'Kitthu, Amaethur 15th, 575 of the 1st Era

SYL'KARA NERVOUSLY thumbed the hematite stone in her pocket, desperately hoping that Nightweaver would hear her pleas and come to her aid. The area was unknown to her and most of the trees looked the same in the dark. She'd heard mention of a village, or city, named Belaigne, but had no clue how far away it was. The only thing she was certain of was that she'd been walking north when she entered the trees, and she only knew that because the sky had been clear enough to catch a quick glimpse of Provoss and Aygos to get her bearings.

The nighttime moons couldn't shine brightly enough to light her way that evening. No amount of elven night vision could quench her desire for daylight. She felt exposed; vulnerable. More-so than she'd ever felt as Johorr's property.

She's a demon! She has to be a demon! Where did she come from? Did Nightweaver set her free? Did Siscci destroy Port Gandraias and send Nightweaver fleeing?

Questions raced through her mind, but she couldn't give them quarter. She couldn't spare the time to stop and think; she had to get away. There could be no distractions, nothing that would allow Siscci or her strange slaves time to catch up with her. Nothing that...

smoke. I smell a fire. Someone is nearby. Perhaps they can help?

She turned east toward the smell, which rode the breeze up from the distant coastal cliffs. It was a guess, as much as anything else, but the direction *felt* right, and her gut hadn't steered her wrong to that point, so she trusted it.

Up ahead stood a cabin. It was old, and slightly worse for wear, but there was smoke escaping the chimney, and that meant warmth. Someone was inside; someone alive who could possibly help. Someone, at least, that could listen to her story and tell her she was crazy; that she hadn't seen what she'd just seen. She desperately hoped that would be the case.

The wooden steps creaked under her meager weight as she ascended. While she was certain whomever lived in the cabin would have heard her footsteps, she took a moment to compose herself and knock, anyway. Her right hand was visibly trembling when she raised it to announce her presence. After a few repetitions, the door creaked open and an old woman peered out to meet her gaze.

"Whaddya want at this time o' night?" demanded the owner.

"Might I sit by your fire and get warm; possibly stay until morning before I continue north in search of aid?" responded Syl'Kara. Her voice cracked and wavered, clearly revealing just how terrified she still was. In truth, it surprised her that she could force the words past her lips at all, let alone voice them clearly.

"By the gods, lass, where be yer shoes? Come on in, you'll catch your death!" belted the woman as she looked Syl'Kara over and swung the door wide.

"Catch my death... such an appropriate turn of phrase," remarked Syl'Kara, brought back to a semblance of emotional normalcy by the irony of the woman's choice of words.

"How'd ye end up way out here? The woods ain't safe this time o' night," said the woman. She guided Syl'Kara to the fireplace, grabbing a blanket off of her chair on the way. Syl'Kara lowered herself to the floor in front of the hearth and slowly rubbed her hands together. The old woman sat on her knees beside her, then thought better of her position and lowered herself the rest of the way to the floor. "Don't know what I were thinkin', my knees ain't what they used ta be."

"Something horrible has happened in Port Gandraias, and Helmdale. I'm running from it, and I need to get out of here. I heard there was a town to the north named Belaigne, and I was *trying* to make it, but..." explained Syl'Kara as best she could. Tears began flowing as thoughts of Thomlin's fate entered her mind. She fell into the old woman's lap as her words faltered, unable to hold her composure any longer. Her fear had subsided, and in its place was a ball of sorrow, slowly growing and threatening to overwhelm her.

"Oh, dear, but yer just a pup aren't ye? You should be with yer parents, far from this wretched place. My husband used ta say, '*taint nuthin good 'bout the north 'cept tha northerners.*' He stayed for the people he loved, not the place. When he passed, I kept our place cause I had nuthin' else. This ain't no place for a young, beautiful girl like you," she added, gently stroking Syl'Kara's hair out of her face with the back of her fingers.

"You sleep now, deary. You can have my lap 'til my legs freeze up, then I'll move ya to my bed. I'll fry ya up some grub in the mornin' and we'll walk ta Belaigne together. That sound a'right?" suggested the lady.

Syl'Kara gently nodded and closed her eyes tighter as tears ran down her cheeks, hoping beyond hope that her dreams wouldn't be of what she'd just witnessed, and thankful beyond measure for the kindness of the stranger she'd stumbled upon.

∴∴∴

SYL'KARA WOKE the next morning in an over-sized bed with a very lumpy hay mattress. Never in her life had she slept as deeply, or for as long, as she had that night. She could feel her feet wrapped in fur under the blankets. It was a strange feeling, considering she hadn't worn anything on them for decades. As she moved to uncover herself, she accidentally kicked several small rocks at the foot of the bed, clanking them together.

She climbed out of bed, slightly confused... until a memory struck. *Geela and Helena used to warm stones by the hearth and place them in our beds to keep us warm at night.* It was oddly comforting to think the woman cared for a stranger so much as to give up her own bed and go to such great lengths. She didn't know how to take the woman's kindness; it wasn't something she was used to experiencing.

The door creaked ever so slightly on its hinges as Syl'Kara nudged it open. The old woman was fast asleep in a chair in front of the fire, a few feet away. She seemed much older than a typical human's lifespan, from her experience, but not nearly as old as Nightweaver had appeared to be. Her hair was a mix of gray and black. It was curly and bushy, with little wisps of straight hair poking through at odd intervals. Her face and hands spoke of long years exposed to the elements. The woman had certainly lived a long and full life.

Almost an hour later, the woman woke to the smell of Syl'Kara's cooking and moaned her approval as she stretched, her joints popping as her tension released. "I said I were gonna cook *you* dawnfry, deary!"

"I wanted to thank you for helping me," said Syl'Kara. "I hope you don't mind," she added, turning to face the woman.

"I don't mind. Finish up so we can get ta Belaigne and find yer help," said the woman as she stood and moved toward the table. As she neared the wood stove, Syl'Kara turned away from her to continue stirring the buttered eggs she was making. The tatters of her shirt and the scarred skin underneath were clearly visible for the first time in the light of day. "Oh my word, lil one. Who did this to ye?"

"Up until yesterday, I was slave to a man named Johorr. He's dead now, or at least I think he is," she explained as she stirred.

"So you don't have no mama? No papa?"

"Not that I ever met," she answered as she began to plate their food. "I was left with a human family because I'm a halfling; the wrong kind of halfling to be raised by the Afyr, and my Dynar father was long gone."

She brought the plates to the table and insisted the old woman sit, rather than inspect the scars from her beatings. They ate in silence for a short time. When the woman decided it had been long enough, she reached over and placed a hand atop Syl'Kara's.

"What hap'ned? You can tell me."

"I've been a slave for twenty years. I could have freed myself and run away, but there was a boy named Thomlin with us. I didn't want to leave him behind. I'm not really an adult yet, by elven standards, and Thomlin is mute. I couldn't imagine us getting very far on our own with no weapons, no coin, barely any clothes, and no experience out in the world or any real education to speak of.

"So, we stayed. We took the beatings, and we stayed," she said, choking back the growing knot in her throat at the thought of Thomlin. "I'm going through a growth spurt; hopefully my last. So, I actually sleep like a human would, for now at least. I woke up two nights ago to a strange sound in the distance. It was... like a cannon firing. Very loud. It echoed through the trees.

"When I looked for the cause of the sound, there was a strange, bright light a good distance away. It was very eerie, and there was an energy in the air that felt unnatural. Johorr and Thomlin slept through it, so I kept the news to myself. Johorr would've thought I was making it up to get attention, anyway.

"The next day we encountered a very, very, *very* old woman on the road. She paid Johorr for a meal, so we camped early. After he drank himself to sleep, she talked for a bit, asking strange questions. I don't think she knew where she was, or the state of the world. To be truthful, I didn't understand why she would've asked the things she did.

"After a bit of conversation, though, I figured out who she was, and it was terrifying. She was the Night Witch, but she referred to herself as Nightweaver," explained Syl'Kara.

"The Night Witch were here?" gasped the woman.

"She was in Port Gandraias. She warned us away from going there, in fact. But, she left us that night and—Johorr being Johorr—we went anyway. The... the whole city had been turned to ash. The people, I mean. Most of the buildings are still standing, but there was this one inn, that-"

"Turned to ash?" asked the woman with panic in her voice.

"Yes. There were little piles of ash everywhere. I found a ring in one. Johorr found a few useless trinkets in several others. Each pile of ash used to be a person. It was horrible, like they all just fell into ash where they stood. And Thomlin... he found a cellar door under a pile of debris at the old inn.

"We found a woman inside. Well, what we thought was a woman. She was wearing several layers of black silk and a pearl mask. We couldn't see any of her features, but... Thomlin was instantly smitten, and Johorr not long after. They both changed. They're not themselves anymore. Thomlin can even speak now, as if his body was new, or fixed," said Syl'Kara. Her cheeks were damp with tears she hadn't realized were falling, and her voice was wavering.

"She changed them?" gasped the woman. Syl'Kara nodded while wiping her face on her sleeves.

"We went to Helmdale next because that's what Siscci wanted, or so Johorr said. That's what they call the strange woman; Siscci. Anyway, we arrived in Helmdale and checked into the inn. The owner took me out back to the servants' entrance and fed me, while the whole town—and more—gathered inside around Siscci.

"I was done eating and saw her taking a man upstairs, so I climbed up to the balcony to see what she was doing with him.

That's when I saw..."

"It's okay. Take yer time. Tell me what you saw."

"She took her mask off, and this horrible demonic face was underneath. He wrinkled up and died while this strange green energy flowed out of his mouth and into hers. Then she made these sounds and red energy jumped out of her and... laid down inside the man's corpse. He healed completely, stood up, and said, 'As *you* *wish*'. That's when I ran, and found your cabin."

"I've seen a fair bit o' strange things in my years. Goblins, kobolds, centaur, minotaur, all manner of thing. Sammy n' I used ta travel a lot in our youth. Things got tough, though, so we moved up here ta be near his mama. I ain't ne'er seen the likes o' what you described. I believe you saw what ye saw, but it's a lot ta take in."

"I just want to get as far away from here as I can. Thomlin is... he's..."

"You think she did ta him what she did ta that man you saw?"

"Yes. So, there's nothing keeping me with Johorr any longer. I need to get south, but it's too far without food and someone to help protect the camp. If I wasn't going through a growth spurt, I could meditate and travel alone, but sleeping—deep sleeping—is too dangerous by myself."

"Belaigne," said the woman, nodding. "That's why ye want to go to Belaigne."

"In hopes that someone could help supply me, or that there might be a merchant traveling south that I could accompany, yes."

"Why not stay in Belaigne, or here... with me?"

"It's not far enough away. I don't think Siscci is going to stop in Helmdale."

"It just dawned on me, we ain't been introduced!" said the woman excitedly. "Name's Aggie," she said, sticking out her hand.

"Syl'Kara," she answered, grasping Aggie's hand in greeting.

"Well, Sylk," said Aggie as she stood. "Let's get you ta Belaigne."

"Sylk... I like that," she said with a smile.

∴ ∴ ∴

THE WOODS were much different in the day than they had been the night before. Parts were still fairly dark due to shade from the canopy above, but there were at least rays of bright light peaking through and casting a faint glow upon everything she could see. The world sounded alive. Birds were singing, insects were buzzing, a small animal scampered off a short distance away and if she listened closely, she could hear a woodpecker rapidly digging its way into a distant tree.

Aggie led her down a path that was sprinkled with pebbles. The occasional flat stone still poked through the moss and clover in places, revealing the path had once been paved and well tended.

"If I'm right, you're leading us west. Might I ask why? I thought Belaigne was north."

"Oh it is, dear, but there's a small lake northwest o' here. That flows into a creek, which drops into a crevice where an old mine shaft opened up many a year ago; long a'fore the Dwarves left fer Skain."

"There were Dwarves here?"

"Oh yes, deary. Many a decade ago, back in my grand-pappy's time. Well, when he were a child. They used ta live in mines 'neath Belaigne and Helmdale, but one day they jus' packed up n' left. No one knows why. Some say they got sick o' the cold. Can't say I blame 'em.

"Besides, we don't wanna go walkin' through miles o' woods when the road is so nearby n' faster."

"Oh. That makes sense," agreed Sylk.

"Belaigne's only a couple hour walk from Helmdale, and I live smack dab in tha middle. We'll be there a'fore ye know it."

"Thank you for everything, Aggie."

"So... you really think that were the Night Witch ye met? I mean, a demon is hard enough ta believe. But she... she ain't s'posed to actually exist."

"Oh, she exists. I don't think the tales are accurate, but she's real. Very real... and terrifying."

"Is it true she can control the darkness?"

"She healed Thomlin's wounds with a simple hand gesture, and surrounded our camp with a protective barrier using no more than a twitch of a finger. I felt an energy coming off of her like the event the night before. I think she caused what happened in Port Gandraias." Chills ran down her spine just talking about the ancient witch. She immediately wanted to change the subject.

"If she turned a city to ash, why weren't you harmed?"

"I don't think we mattered to her. We... just happened to be there. So, she bartered for a meal and asked a few questions, then left."

"She just walked off?"

"She vanished. She was there one second, and gone the next as if she'd never been there. Thomlin and Johorr didn't even remember her."

"I see," said Aggie. The extra wrinkles on her forehead indicated she was trying to put the pieces together.

"I can't know for sure, but I think *whatever* happened in the port woke Siscci, or freed her. She was underground, in some kind of cellar. I've been in the back rooms of that inn, making food for Johorr and helping clean up. I never saw a cellar door, so I'm not sure where it came from, or where it was hidden. Clearly something secret was going on."

"Here we are," said Aggie as she came to a stop at the edge of the main road.

Sylk had been so caught up in her thoughts, and her story, that their walk had gone by in what felt like seconds. She hadn't even realized they were approaching the road until she found herself standing on it.

"Do I just head north from here?" asked Sylk.

"*We* head north from here. I'm not abandoning you to the wilds, deary," said Aggie as she pulled Sylk into an embrace. "You ain't gotta be alone no more, youngin."

"Ho there! Identify yourselves!" yelled a strange voice.

∴ ∴ ∴

SYLK AND Aggie looked toward the sound of the voice to see five armed guards approaching. The one in the lead was wearing a suit of chain armor that appeared custom made, and expensive. It was old and had seen a lot of use, revealing her to be the veteran among them. An old scar ran down her face from just above her left eyebrow to below her chin. Her lower jaw tilted in such a way that indicated her wound had been very deep and not properly tended or healed.

The leader's hair was close cropped and partially gray. Her face had a no nonsense air about it, and her piercing gaze made Sylk feel more than a little uneasy. To her left and right were a pair of middle-aged men, both a little worse for wear but fairly healthy. They seemed as if they could handle themselves, if push came to shove, but they appeared to prefer the company of ale to their swords.

Two teenage boys brought up the rear of their formation,

both fidgeting to keep their ill-fitting armor in place as they tried to keep up with their very determined leader. Sylk assumed they were last-minute conscripts, hired in a hurry for whatever mission they'd embarked on, and hadn't had time to find proper equipment for the journey.

"I said identify yourselves!" barked the female soldier. They came to a halt directly in front of the pair of confused women.

"Oh, stop it Jae. Ye know who I am," said Aggie.

"Aggie? Sorry, it's been a *long* time. Where've you been?" said Rae, her voice noticeably lighter and less stern.

"I've been in my cabin, ya dolt. Where else would I be?"

"Well, you don't come into town anymore for supplies, so-"

"I grow everything I need. Besides, ye folk talk too much," chuckled Aggie.

"Who's this with you?"

"My name is Syl'Kara, but you can call me Sylk," she answered, casting a smile of thanks toward Aggie for the nickname.

"What brings you two out on the road? There's been some trouble of late, and we were just heading to Helmdale to check it out," explained Jae. "It seems a lot of folk from Belaigne went to Helmdale last night and never returned."

"Something horrible is happening in Helmdale. I ran last night trying to find Belaigne to seek aid. But, I don't know the area and I found Aggie's cabin instead."

"Tell us what's happening," demanded Jae. She grabbed Sylk's arm and yanked her toward Helmdale as she went to walk past.

"What are you doing?" gasped Sylk.

"We're on our way to Helmdale. You claim to know what's going on, so you can explain on the way."

"I don't want to go back to Helmdale!"

"She's a slave, ma'am," stated one of the middle-aged men as Sylk's back spun to face him.

"A run-away slave claiming there's trouble in Helmdale and several missing citizens of Belaigne, all on the same day? No, this isn't a coincidence. You're coming with us," ordered Jae.

"I thought Tellrindos didn't condone slavery? Why would you take me back to him?" asked Sylk, with more than a little panic in her voice.

"Oh, we'll deal with that when we arrive. *After* we find out where our citizens have gone, and *after* you've explained what's going on.

Don't bother lying to me, either. I'll know if you do."

"Jae, she's a sweet girl. Ye don't have ta handle her that way," urged Aggie.

Jae let go of Sylk's arm for Aggie's benefit, then turned to face the old woman. "She's your responsibility, then. If she runs off before I have my answers, you'll find yourself behind bars. Is that understood?"

"Why are ye being this way?" demanded Aggie.

"A lot of things have changed since you became a recluse. The whole town depends on me for protection, and two dozen people just up and vanished last night after some strange boy came riding in on a horse from Helmdale, talking about some '*Answer to all our prayers.*' So, duty must come first; pleasantries second."

"I'll just have to talk to Lord Penrin 'bout this then, won't I?" said Aggie.

"After this is over with you can talk to his tombstone all you like."

"Penrin's dead?" gasped Aggie.

"Lady Milfirth is in charge now, ma'am," answered the other older man.

"How long have I been gone?" wondered Aggie.

"Five years, Aggie," answered Jae. "Now, get a move on," she finished, pointing south.

∴∴∴

SYLK WASN'T sure that any of the guards believed her story. She had to admit it was fairly far-fetched. Besides, they had no reason to trust her. The teenage boys that traveled with Jae seemed uneasy at the conclusion of her tale, but the other two men almost looked like they were about to laugh. Jae, herself, was impossible to read.

By the time the tale had concluded, Helmdale's outskirts were within sight. From that distance, everything seemed normal. Sylk secretly wondered how many of the residents were now slaves to Siscci, or new versions of themselves, or whatever it was the demon was doing to them. She suddenly had a thought. She'd forgotten to explain *how* Siscci was manipulating everyone.

"Wait!" she blurted, coming to a stop in front of them. Jae went to walk past her, seeming not to care about any further details. "She uses some kind of mind control. Men, women... anyone that gets close to Siscci seems to fall under a spell; as if all they can imagine is having sex with her, and nothing else matters."

"Then how did you get away?" asked one of the men.

Jae stopped and turned to face the young elven girl. Her face said she had listened long enough and would hear no more. "If that's true, why not *begin* your story with that detail?" asked Jae.

"I don't know how it works. She almost had control of me, but I was able to resist her. I don't know why, I-" she explained. Jae turned to walk away again in the middle of her sentence. "I'm not making this up!"

"We'll see for ourselves, lass," remarked one of the men. They barged past her, unwilling to let her warnings stop them.

"Come now, they'll see soon enough," said Aggie, urging her to follow the guards. "If yer right, we'll flee as ye did a'fore. If yer wrong, and we don't follow, we'll go ta prison."

Sylk sighed and turned back toward Helmdale. She knew they were walking into a disastrous situation, but felt powerless to convince them.

∴ ∴ ∴

FROM OUTSIDE of town, Helmdale seemed vacant. No guards stood at the gates to the center of town, no citizens buzzed along the street tending their daily business. It seemed as if everyone had simply vanished. Jae and her men drew their swords, ready for anything to jump out at them at any time. They walked cautiously down the street, inspecting every window, door, and alley.

Sylk slipped off on her own, following a few seconds behind up against the buildings on their left, ready to duck into an alley, through a window, or through a door at a moment's notice. She didn't trust the eerie silence. The fear she'd left behind when she fled the town the night before was slowly creeping its way back in and taking over.

Aggie stayed a few feet behind the guards, peering over their shoulders and between them intermittently, trying to catch a glimpse of what might lie ahead. She seemed apprehensive, but otherwise unphased by the surrounding silence.

As the group rounded the corner, the inn came into view at the far end of the street. People were sitting on the ground all around the entrance; on the porch, in the street, and in the dirt beside the building. Jae stopped for a moment and seemed perplexed. None of the citizens made any attempt to acknowledge their presence. It was as if they were all in a trance.

Jae approached cautiously, her guards spread out to her sides. Aggie stood in the middle of the street, watching intently. Sylk ducked behind a wooden bench and peered out over the arm, hoping she wouldn't get caught by Siscci's servants.

Siscci exited the building. She seemed to glide across the porch, down the steps, and onto the ground. Her movement was graceful beyond anything they'd ever witnessed, and her form as elusive to identify as Sylk had described. A sense of dread washed over Jae, and her face tensed in response. She raised her sword into a more defensive position and pressed on.

"She's so beautiful," said one of the young guards, barely louder than a whisper.

One of the older guards jumped forward and put his off-hand on Jae's shoulder. "Let's just put our swords away."

"What are you-" Jae started. She turned her head to face the man and could see his eyes filled with lust and wonder. A quick glance around told her that all of her companions were similarly enthralled. "Fuck!"

Jae spun free of the man's grasp and readied herself, slowly backing away. The first man lunged forward, sword raised high, swinging downward. She stepped aside at the last second, and dragged the center of her blade across his hips, just below his leather breastplate. His innards began to spill through the opening as he desperately dropped his sword, fell to his knees, and clamored to shove them back inside. She stepped past the fallen man and parried attacks from the other older guard, and one of the younger, in rapid succession.

Sylk watched in horror as the guards began fighting amongst themselves. She looked at Siscci in panic. The creature was slowly approaching, hands outstretched to her sides toward the ground, moaning in a strange language while dark purple energies radiated from her pearlescent mask.

Aggie shrieked and ran back the way they'd come, as fast as her aging body would allow. Several enthralled citizens got off the ground by the inn and ran down an alley in the same direction, clearly intent on cutting the old woman off before she could get away.

Jae dispatched the second experienced warrior with a parry that sent his weapon wide, turning her sword in mid-swing and thrusting it abruptly through his exposed neck. She spun quickly to face the two young soldiers directly, but not before each of their blades bashed into her chainmaille breastplate, sending pain radiating through her torso.

She drove her left heel into the side of one boy's knee, buckling it inward and sending him crashing into the other boy. With a thrust and a slash as they fell, she stabbed the first boy in the face and sliced into the second boy's upper chest. The last victim's arm came down atop her blade before she could pull it free, jarring it out of her grasp and taking it to the ground with him.

Jae turned toward Siscci in a hurry, trying to see where her quarry had gone. Siscci stood inches away looking up at her; hands outstretched and moaning. Jae drew her dagger and thrust it toward the small demon, but narrowly missed. The weapon appeared to strike precisely where she intended; the left side of the creature's chest. At the last second, the blade seemed to pass through a shimmering layer of her silken garb, hitting nothing but air. It was as if Siscci wasn't truly standing where she appeared to be standing, or as if her clothing was causing such an effect.

Try as she might—sending one attack after another—she could not seem to wound her target. The creature seemed to be everywhere but where she was standing, and yet—by all appearances—had not moved an inch.

Siscci's arms shot upward in a flash. She grabbed Jae's face between her hands and shrieked a horrible, ear piercing cry. Blood streaked down the sides of Jae's head, rolling over Siscci's fingers like a thin, crimson waterfall. Jae thrust the dagger in desperation toward the demon's heart, but Siscci drove her left hand down and toward center just fast enough to knock the weapon free, shattering Jae's wrist in the process.

As the dagger skittered across the ground, Siscci's hand returned to Jae's head, and she pulled the seasoned warrior down to meet her gaze. Their foreheads touched as Jae struggled to break free of her grip. A wave of energy pulsed through Jae, instantly calming her as if she were in a trance.

Siscci released Jae's face, leaving her hunched over and frozen in place. She backed away a step and seemed to calm. Several of the citizens stood and walked over to join them, then dragged Jae toward the inn without a word. She stood for a moment in the center of the road, peering down at the corpses of the other guards before joining her servants at the inn.

DESPERATION

Ris'Gaula, Amaethur 16th, 575 of the 1st Era

WHEN THE road appeared to be clear, Sylk came out from behind the wooden bench and crawled as fast as she could across the ground to retrieve Jae's dagger, which had slid to a stop nearby. She turned as fast as possible and got back to the building, then looked around quickly to see if anyone had noticed her.

Getting out of town was the only thought on her mind until she heard Aggie scream from across town. With her heart beating so hard and fast that she could hear it in her eardrums, she ran down the alley to the rear of the main street and turned left toward the source of the sound.

Two men were holding Aggie by her arms, dragging her feet behind them as they half-carried her toward Siscci. She was squirming so much they didn't notice the tiny elf closing in on them, brandishing a weapon.

Sylk closed on the men and quickly drove her dagger into the chest of the man on the left. It went in far easier than she'd expected, sinking into his flesh and passing between his ribs with little resistance, thanks to her momentum. He gasped and reached for the dagger's hilt, releasing Aggie in the process. Sylk released the dagger out of shock; completely surprised by how easy it was to end the man's life, and how quickly it had all happened.

The second man jerked Aggie backward, sending her crashing to the ground behind him. He jumped forward and sent a fist flying toward Sylk's head. She ducked beneath his attack with relative ease, being smaller and faster. As he corrected his positioning and spun to attack again, she reached down and retrieved her blade from the first victim, then turned to face him.

She slashed wildly in the air between them, driving him backward in a frantic attempt to avoid being haphazardly sliced. Aggie got to her feet and moved toward them, intent on tackling the man to the ground. As she arrived, he jumped back, grabbed her by the neck, and used her own momentum to pull her between himself and the crazed elf.

Sylk's dagger struck Aggie accidentally, cutting deep into her lower neck. She shrieked and released the blade, but the damage had already been done. Aggie fell backward into the man, sending them both to the ground. The horror at what she'd just done was quickly overcome by pure, unadulterated anger at the man who had forced her hand.

As he crashed to the ground beneath Aggie, Sylk took advantage of his prone state and jumped atop them both. She retrieved the dagger that was hanging loosely out of Aggie's flesh, then leaned over the old woman and peered directly into the man's hazy, enthralled eyes.

Seething with anger and fear, she slowly sank the dagger into the man's left eye. It didn't go in as far as she'd expected, stopping as it met the bone at the rear of his eye socket. He wailed in pain, but was unable to retaliate or prevent her assault due to the weight of the women atop him. She left the dagger embedded in his eye, raised both hands into a single clenched fist, and drove them down onto the weapon's rounded pommel.

A resounding crunch echoed off the building beside them as the dagger buried crossguard-deep into the man's skull.

Sylk climbed off the pile and frantically tried to stop the blood that was gushing out of Aggie's neck with each beat of her heart. Aggie slowly reached up and stroked Sylk's cheek as if to say, 'It's okay, *deary*,' before her arm went limp and fell to the ground with a thud.

"No!" cried Sylk as tears streaked through the dust on her cheeks. She wiped at her face to clear away the signs of her grief, forgetting that Aggie's blood was all over them.

Four hands latched onto Sylk's arms from behind, bringing her sorrow to an abrupt and unexpected halt. She was too short to flail and break free as they carried her, several inches off the ground, toward the inn.

So this is how it ends?

∴ ∴ ∴

THE CAPTORS tossed Sylk to the floor in Siscci's room, sending her into a near-collision with Jae. The soldier was being kept on her knees by two men, while a third held a dagger near her throat.

"Good. You made it," joked Jae. The men pushed down harder on her shoulders, while the third pressed his dagger firmly against her neck, drawing a thin line of blood to the surface.

Two other men dragged Sylk to the other side of Jae, and pushed her into a similar position on the floor next to her, though they didn't bother placing a dagger to her throat. Sylk assumed this was because she was so much smaller, and considered far less a threat. After all, she hadn't attacked their master.

The men held them in that position for what must have been hours. Night fell before they heard any movement outside the room. Neither of them were certain where Siscci was, and their routine glances at one another confirmed what both were thinking. *The longer this takes, the worse it's going to be.*

"Why are you doing this?" demanded Jae.

As if on queue, Siscci entered the room. A wave of silence washed over them. Neither Siscci's footsteps nor Jae's verbal outburst seemed to make a sound. Once the demon arrived before them, she bent at the hip and stared directly into Jae's eyes, then Sylk's.

She stood and turned away from them, as if unconcerned by their presence. Slowly, she slipped the loops at the ends of her silken garb off of her fingers and toes. As she moved, Sylk noticed tiny rips and tears across the garment.

Jae's dagger did hit her!

Siscci carefully disrobed and placed each layer of her clothing over the bed, one beside the other. As the layers came off, her putrid, leathery flesh came into view. Her skin was brown with patches and hints of red. To Sylk it looked as if she were both decaying and healing simultaneously, as sections of her back seemed to ooze a clear slime and shift from red to brown, while others dried up and turned red. Over and over, the pattern repeated, no portion of her skin remaining a single color for longer than a few seconds.

Small black spikes lined the demon's spine from hip to neck. Tiny, curved spikes protruded from her shoulders at random angles, as if someone had driven them into her flesh rather than them growing naturally. Only the creature's hands and feet looked like a normal human. The rest of her was horrifying to see, and the smell that radiated off her was akin to sulfur and wet ash.

Finally, she removed the pearlescent mask and placed it beside the rest of her garb. Jae cast Sylk a sidelong glance as the creature waved its hands slowly over the clothing. The elven girl was nearly paralyzed with fear, and didn't blink through the entire process. It was then that Jae considered the possibility that they might not escape the encounter alive.

"What are you going to do with us?" demanded Jae.

Siscci continued using her magic to mend the garments damaged by Jae's dagger, and made no attempt to answer for herself. One of her servants answered in her stead.

"You will feed her once she is finished fixing what you've done," he said.

"Feed her? I'm not a cook. She'd be better off eating that mattress," joked Jae.

"You misunderstand. We don't eat... food," said the man with an eerie smile.

"We?" asked Jae, peering deep into the man's eyes.

"We," he answered with a nod.

"So you're all like she is?"

"Soon."

"Fuck," sighed Jae. The man smiled at her dismay and stood up straight. "You better thank me for this," Jae said to Sylk.

Jae drove her torso backward, away from the knife at her throat, wedging her head between the two men behind her. She twisted with all her might, rolling out from under the downward force their hands exerted on her shoulders and through the legs of the man nearest the door, away from Sylk.

Siscci turned to face the commotion and took a few steps toward Jae. The two men holding Sylk jumped to assist the others, grabbing at Jae's legs.

Sylk watched for a split second, then realized what Jae was doing. Biting back against her instincts—and the fear that was driving them—she jumped to her feet and scooped up all of Siscci's silk clothing.

As the men reacted and tried to reach for her, she ran toward the big window she'd peered through the day before, and dove toward it, spinning in the air so her back would take the brunt of the collision. She landed on her side on the small balcony as shards of glass flew all around her.

Sylk got to her feet just enough to stumble to the railing and allow herself to tumble over. After crashing down onto the servant's table below, she rolled toward the ground. She landed on her knees, right shoulder, and part of her face, completely out of breath.

She gasped and inhaled as deeply as she could. The pain in her back and right side were overwhelming, but she didn't have any time to spare. She did her best to ignore everything her body was telling her, and ran as fast as she could into the dark night beyond the dim light seeping out of the inn's windows.

∴ ∴ ∴

EVERY STEP sent searing pain through her hips and lower back. Each twist of her torso shifted her shirt, causing it to bump against, or tug upon, the shards of glass and splinters that protruded from her flesh. Even the act of breathing filled her with pain and was difficult to accomplish.

Though not trained in the medical arts, she was fairly confident she'd sustained several broken ribs, possibly a broken hip, and far too many lacerations and torn muscles to count. All she wanted to do was stop moving, lie down and succumb to her pain. The cries of alarm that rang out behind her insisted that she had to keep moving if she wanted to live, so she soldiered on.

Sylk had no idea where she was going, other than away from Helmdale. She had an inkling that she was perhaps heading east, toward the cliffs at the edge of the Hystari, but there was no way for her to be certain. She'd never learned proper nighttime navigation, and even if she had, the sky was overcast and barely visible through the trees. Her only hope was that her head start would be enough, and that Siscci's re-made humans couldn't see in the dark as clearly as an elf.

She looked down at the bundle of black silk in her arms as she stumbled through the underbrush, curious if she should put it on. The distraction caused her to ricochet off a tree, sending a new wave of pain through the left side of her body.

No, I can't wear this until I get the glass and wood out of my back, or it'll just tear and then it wouldn't help me at all.

Grabbing the gear had been an act of desperation. There hadn't been a plan, or the privacy required to formulate one. Jae's self sacrifice was just as sudden to her as it was to their captors. When she got up to flee, Siscci's gear had been convenient to grab on her way out. She hoped that taking it would both hinder the demon and help in her own defense should they confront one another in the future.

Maybe it'll help me survive if we come face to face. Maybe it won't. But at least the townsfolk will have to see her for what she is. She can't hide behind a silken veil, now that I've taken it. Maybe some of them will break free of her control and fight back.

She knew it was wishful thinking, but at the same time, she couldn't determine any other options.

Distracted again, she barreled haphazardly between two trees... straight into a thorn bush. She yelped in pain involuntarily, but quickly recovered her composure. The world around her went deathly silent. She stood still, waiting, as small specks of blood formed around the thorns that still punctured her flesh.

"This way!" yelled a man that was alarmingly close.

Sylk's skin went cold as panic and adrenaline coursed through her anew. She backed out of the bush as fast as she could, turned, and ran with renewed focus. The pain was slowly being drowned out by her desire to survive.

I've got to find somewhere to hide! And I have to get my hands free to do that.

After a few seconds of careful consideration, she decided it was worth the risk to stop for a moment and attempt to stow the bundle of silk. She squatted and frantically laid the pieces of black cloth on the ground atop one another, then folded the pile into as small a square as she could manage. After the bundle was prepared, she tucked it into her tunic and under the band of cloth she used to protect her breasts. Once it was secure, she adjusted her tunic to cover the silk and stood back up with her hands free.

She glanced over her shoulder for a second and caught sight of someone moving through the brush a few dozen yards away. They passed in and out of sight, weaving between trees but heading in her general direction. With no more time to spare, she turned and ran. Having her hands and arms free, she was able to better maintain her balance and move much faster than when she initially entered the forest.

A few minutes later, she leaped over a small log and found herself standing in a tiny clearing. Two deer, startled by her arrival, whipped their heads toward her and went into a panic. They fled to her right, crashing through the underbrush. The sound of their egress echoed through the night, alerting the men that followed her.

"Over there!" shouted a man.

How are they moving so fast? Am I that slowed by my injuries?

Her heart was beating so fast that she half expected it to burst. She was out of breath, slowly being overcome by pain, and losing far too much blood to keep going for much longer. With her options dwindling by the second, she quickly looked at the edge of the clearing for a place to hide. She found a small patch of bushes a short distance away, surrounded by wild strawberries and ivy.

She ran near her chosen hiding place, but past it, making sure to leave prints that they would easily find. When she'd gone a few dozen yards in the wrong direction, she carefully backtracked, walking backwards in the same footprints she'd left behind. Once she was back at the edge of the clearing, she carefully made her way to the bushes, stepping on stumps, stones, twigs, small patches of ivy, and other plant-life in an attempt to hide her new prints.

Once she reached the far side of the bush, she lowered herself to the ground and crawled inside. The branches skipped and skittered into her back as she moved, snagging on several large chunks of glass and wood still sticking out of her wounds. She winced in pain, but made sure not to succumb to it and wail, as her body was insisting she do. One of the larger pieces of glass wiggled free and tumbled to the ground just beside her face. She stopped and looked down at it, instantly filling her with a temporary wave of relief. Any closer and it could have hit her eye on the way to the ground, ending any chance she had of escape.

Two men entered the clearing a few seconds later and stopped to look around. One was shorter than the other, and both were fairly nondescript from her vantage point and distance. The taller one walked away from her, studying the far side of the clearing. The shorter one came toward her and stopped right next to the bush she was under. She held her breath, and tried to calm her heart, so that he wouldn't hear her. His breath was heavy from exertion, and peppered with little huffs and grunts showing his distaste for her escape.

"Anything?" yelled the taller man.

"No," answered the shorter one. His voice sounded familiar. She couldn't be certain, because she'd only heard his voice once, but she thought it might be Thomlin.

"I found some prints. I'll check them out. You keep looking here in case she's hiding," said the taller one as he returned to the center of the clearing.

"Be quick," said the shorter man. His bare feet shuffled around the bush, turning every which way as he circled around it, peering in every direction for any sign of her.

Bare feet? That voice? It has to be Thomlin, she decided.

"What's this?" said Thomlin from behind her.

A cold hand grabbed her ankle and tugged with far more strength than Thomlin had ever had. She grabbed the piece of glass as she slid out of the bush, palming it as best she could. Before she knew it, she was no longer under the bush, and another hand was rolling her over onto her wounded back.

"Gotcha," said Thomlin. His eyes glowed red as he smiled wickedly down at her; the pupils seemed to have split into two thin, vertical lines. He reached down and grabbed her by the shoulders, then lifted her to her feet and peered directly into her eyes. "Don't you want to join us? I know you cared for this man. You can be with him for all eternity, if you just-"

Fear was threatening to paralyze her. Every breath sent waves of pain radiating through her torso, and she found herself increasingly unable to control the frequency and depth of those breaths. Her subconscious insisted that she was about to suffocate, and pushed her to draw more air than she could contain. A hot sensation filled her core, like a ball of anxiousness welling up near her heart, intent on overtaking her.

The man in front of her—speaking to her—was not the Thomlin she knew. It wore his skin, but he was no longer the mute boy that gave his back to save hers; that took beatings from their unreasonable owner on her behalf. Gone was the boy she had once decided to care for.

Her right arm shot upward as fast as her muscles would move it, reaching under his grasp to drive the shard of glass into his neck. It cut deep into his windpipe, stopping his words short and preventing him from breathing or calling out for help. She drove it deeper with the palm of her hand before pulling away, leaving none of it exposed for him to grab and pull free.

He stumbled backward, picking at his throat in a desperate attempt to find whatever it was she'd driven into his neck. She winced in pain as she withdrew her arm from the attack. The motion had moved her shoulder in such a way that the blade ground against a shard of glass and didn't want to go back into position when she returned her arm to her side.

As he fell to the ground, she walked over and climbed atop him, holding his arms down with her knees. She reached her left hand back, retrieved the dagger from his thigh, and placed the tip just under his jaw. With one final motion, she extinguished the spark of life from Thomlin's eyes forever, and the red glow therein went dark.

Sylk pulled the dagger out of his neck and flipped it around. After a few seconds of struggle, she managed to reach back and wedge the tip against the shard of glass in her right shoulder blade. She tensed the muscles of her back despite the pain, and tapped at the glass with the tip of the dagger until she nudged it free.

I'm not going to last much longer, she thought. The pain was subsiding overall, but for a few spikes and pangs accompanying certain movements. She was either getting used to the pain, or her body was on the verge of passing out. She'd heard tell of severe wounds hurting less just before unconsciousness, and the danger that followed such an event. As *if I don't have enough to worry about.*

Without further delay, she climbed off of Thomlin and ran toward what would have been a right turn in comparison to the direction she'd been traveling previously. She didn't know when the other man would return, but she wanted to get as much distance between them as she could before he found Thomlin's body.

.· .· .·

AN HOUR later, she found herself at a hole. It looked more like a gash cut into the ground, or a wound, than it did a natural formation. It was too wide to jump across, but not overly large. There was no sound of rushing water, so it didn't appear as if a river had carved it into the landscape. She didn't know the area, so she wasn't sure how long the hole was, and therefore how long it would take to get around.

Sylk listened for a few minutes, standing on the edge of the cliff. An owl hooted in the distance. A small creature scampered away nearby, likely frightened by the call of its predator. Crickets were singing, and small flying insects were buzzing about. She heard no footsteps of a human following her, and no sounds she could identify as a large animal anywhere nearby.

For the first time in days, she felt safe. Exhausted, filled with physical pain, and on the verge of passing out... but safe.

Clank, clank, echoed a sound from the bottom of the hole. The sound was sudden, and out of place. She let loose a small gasp before catching herself, and covering her mouth out of reflex with her right hand; a movement that sent a fresh wave of pain through her back.

Clank, clank, clank, came the sound again. She was certain it was the sound of metal banging against stone, somewhere down in the depths below.

"Hello?" she said, leaning into the ravine just a touch. No response came. She wasn't sure if there was a person down below, or if she'd spoken loud enough to be heard. Just to make sure, she lowered herself to the ground, moving as gingerly as she could, until she had extended her head out over the opening and could feel comfortable yelling a little more loudly.

"Is anyone down there?" she called.

"Oh, thank Galrath!" said a man's voice. The sound was faint, indicating he was very far below her position. He sounded as if he might have been just as exhausted as she was.

"I need help. I'm being chased by some men, and I'm wounded," she called out.

"I'm stuck down here. I... I have food, and bandages—a whole mess of supplies, really. I'm the only one left down here."

"How bad are you stuck? Can you get out soon? And... where's the exit? I'm leaning over a cliff right now, probably right on top of you."

"Oh? There's a fissure above me, and I can smell the forest on the breeze. I'm in an old dwarven mine. Came here on an expedition, but then part of the mine caved in and killed most of the crew. If you could climb down, and lend a hand, we could get through this debris in a few short hours. If I have to keep digging by myself, this could take days," he explained.

"Climb down? I may not have the strength. My back is terribly wounded, and I'm on the verge of passing out as it is. I'm afraid I might not make it."

"Do you have any rope?"

"No. I was running for my life. I didn't have time to stop and grab one," she said. *It's not like I could've anticipated finding some strange man in a mineshaft in the middle of the woods,* she mused. *But if I could make it down, maybe he could help me close these wounds and give me something to eat. Maybe I'd stand a better chance of surviving the night. It's not like they're going to look for me underground.*

"Let me see if I can find a way down. Be ready to catch me, just in case."

"How am I supposed to know where-"

"Just be ready!"

Sylk inspected the side of the fissure directly below her. She could see a few places she could step, and several roots that would help her navigate at least halfway down into the darkness. The bottom wasn't visible from her vantage point, but if she could hear his voice, she reasoned it couldn't be too much farther than she could see.

With a sigh, she swung her body around so that her feet were pointed toward the opening and slowly lowered herself down to the first foothold. Her arms barely wanted to cooperate with her actions. They seemed fine, strength-wise, when reaching below her waist to find purchase, but the act of lowering her body weight downward was tenuous at best. Her strength seemed to give out halfway through the motion, causing her to come down on her foothold faster, and harder, than she would've liked.

Two of the small cracks she'd planned to use as a foothold gave way under her abrupt landing, leaving her dangling from her fingertips. Each time that happened, her heart went into a panic while she scrambled to find a new toehold. Eventually, she made it to the furthest point she'd seen from above and clung tightly to the wall while she searched for the remainder of her route.

"How are you doing up there?" called the man from below. His voice seemed older now that she was closer and could hear it more clearly.

"I'm fine... just trying to find a way to continue," she answered. More than a little of her pain made it into her tone of voice. Based on the scuffling about she heard below, she assumed he was nervously pacing. "I... don't think I can get much lower. Is there anything you can use to break my fall?" she pleaded.

"See how far you can get. Maybe I can stack some of our supply crates and-"

"I already fell through a window and over a balcony today. I don't think I'll survive another fall like that," she interrupted. Her grip was about to fail; she could feel it in her fingers. She looked around frantically for a lower position she could move to.

"Right, um... I'll gather my expedition's bedrolls. Hang on!"

"That's what I'm doing!"

Sylk saw a few places to grab a bit lower down and carefully made her way to them. She finally reached a point where she could vaguely see the rocky ground below. An old man rushed into view, dragging a few thin padded blankets. He looked up toward her and seemed to be taken aback by what he saw.

"You're Dynar? Are you from Lothenheim?"

"Can we discuss this when I'm on the ground?"

"Oh! Right... let me go grab a sack of bread and put it under the bedding. Hang on." The old man raced off and returned a few seconds later with a large burlap sack filled with loaves of bread. Several spilled out when he laid it down. He then pulled the bedding over top and raised his hands toward her, indicating that she should let go and fall onto the pile. "I'll do my best to catch you, and direct your fall into the pile. You seem small enough, your weight shouldn't be any trouble for me."

She considered her options and couldn't think of any other course of action. That didn't mean she was happy with the idea of dropping down to a stone floor. As much as her fingers and toes were beginning to fail her, they seemed to be refusing to follow her commands to let go.

"Trust me," said the man.

Sylk looked down at the man, waving his hands below her in a vain attempt to say she should hurry up. *What's one more injury,* she decided. Her breath caught in her throat when she let go. The sensation of falling rushed through her gut, accompanied by far more regret than she'd anticipated. Before another thought could cross her mind, she crashed into the poor man's upper body, and then sideways onto the padding he'd placed.

The last thing she saw before she passed out was various shards of bread skittering across the floor.

DISCOVERY

Ris'Uttyr, Amaethur 17th, 575 of the 1st Era

FOR THE second time in as many days, Sylk awoke in a strange bed. She was lying on her stomach atop the padding on the ground, in the same place she'd landed when she fell. Her back didn't hurt nearly as much as it had before her fall. In fact, she felt rather good, all things considered.

She looked around for a moment, and caught sight of the man sitting off to one side, eating a hunk of bread and a piece of dried meat. "Could I have some food as well? I haven't eaten since yesterday morning." Her stomach grumbled as if to accentuate her point.

"You're awake! I'm so glad you made it," he said. His smile couldn't have stretched any further if it tried. His white hair and beard stood out in the dark cave, easily reflecting the limited light that reached them from above. He leaned over and handed her what remained of the dried meat in his hand, and a fresh piece of bread from the bag she was lying on. "You can roll over and sit up, if you like. I've tended your wounds.

"Lucky you, we came down here fully supplied. Though I'll admit, I used up what remained of our healing potions fixing those wounds all over your back, hips, and shoulders. I had to wait til the sun was high enough to light the fissure to see all the pieces of glass in your back, and pull them out. I guess it's also lucky for you that I happen to have a fair collection of rather delicate tools with me, thanks to my job. If I were a typical miner, there's no way I could've helped you."

Sylk rolled over and slid off the pile of bread and bedding toward the man. She sat on the stone and gently leaned back, testing her strength and the state of her injuries. He had, apparently, done an amazing job of healing her. She took a bite of the bread and gave him a nod of thanks. He waited patiently for her to swallow before resuming the conversation.

"Thank you for helping me, sir. Once I rest a bit and give my body time to digest your gracious offering, I'll gladly help dig us out of here," she said.

"I find it strange to encounter someone way out here. Let alone a Dynar with white hair. Are you, perhaps, a halfling? Part Afyr, I reckon?"

"I am," she answered between bites. "I was raised by humans near Uldenheim, and sold into slavery some twenty years ago. My master traveled to Port Gandraias for trade, and we found the city decimated. We made our way to Helmdale with this strange survivor of the port, and I've been on the run ever since."

"How did you come by all the glass and splinters in your back?"

"Let me finish this meal and I'll explain everything," she said. She hoped he would be understanding enough to comply. *Who am I to make such demands?*

"Oh, certainly. You eat up, we have plenty of time." He resumed eating his own meal, and remained quiet throughout. Aside from the occasional smile in her direction, he allowed her to eat in peace and made no attempt to pressure her further.

When they completed their meal, Sylk explained the series of events that led her to the fissure in excruciating detail. He hung on her every word, never once questioning even the strangest, most unbelievable parts of the story. As she finally arrived at her plummet into the fissure, he allowed his face to reveal his true feelings about her story. He wasn't in disbelief if she could read him properly. From what she could tell, he seemed to be very upset.

"Do you know where we are?" he asked. "Where this fissure is located?" he added, waving at the gaping hole above their heads.

"No, sir. I don't have a clue."

"We are approximately a two-hour walk northeast of Port

Gandraias. If you'd been able to cross it, you'd have found the edge of the forest no more than an hour south of here, and easy access to the city, and the sea, or roads south from there."

"But how?"

"It's simply the way the terrain works in these parts. The road takes a longer route than you'd expect, because it goes around several of these fissures all across the area; some are quite a bit larger than this one. Going through the forest is a much more direct route, if one could cross the fissures safely, or find a good place to pass between them."

"Either way, there's no help to be found in the port. Nightweaver turned everyone to ash."

"True, but there's a relevance to our location that you aren't yet aware of. You see, my excavation and study was occurring beneath the city. Here... follow me, and I'll show you. There's something you need to see."

∴ ∴ ∴

THE OLD man led Sylk into a large room, carved out of a cavern in the far distant past. Someone long ago had covered the walls in strange writings and pictures, carved into the stone with precision and patience. At the far end of the chamber stood a black stone wall, and at its center was a great stone door standing ajar with a pile of dirt and dust heaped in front of it.

"My name is Jareth Lahn. I am a historian and scribe, and I work for the Laethan family, a noble house in Lothenheim. I was studying old land claims in the city archive, and stumbled across a Laethan claim to these mines. They sent me here with a team of miners and stonecutters to inspect the mines, with the sole purpose of identifying which section of the mines the family actually owned, and if they'd be worth reopening. There's a dispute amongst the noble houses over who owns what down here, and whether it's even worth the legal battle to pursue enforcing their claims."

"I thought you said these were dwarven mines?"

"They were! The dwarves who now live in Skain used to live down here. They left nearly two centuries ago, and never really said why. According to the paperwork I found, they simply claimed the mines had run dry and sold the land off to the noble houses to fund their journey to some new city they'd discovered, far off in Pelrigoss.

"For whatever reason, nobody ever thought to come and *check* on the mines to see if they were telling the truth. I guess relying on the dwarves for all of our mining for hundreds of years wasn't the wisest course of action, because it wasn't until the past few decades that we humans started learning the craft for ourselves; and even then, they focused on strip-mining the surface, rather than venturing down here.

"But, I don't think the dwarves left because they ran out of things to mine. Here, let me show you." He used a small piece of flint and steel to light a reed and then used that to light several oil lamps positioned around the chamber.

"Notice the large, plain wall. No carvings or writings to be found here. Nothing of note, really, aside from the *type* of stone it is, and the door at the center. And if you step this way, you'll notice the door is several feet thick. The chamber beyond has no other exit, and if the walls at the front are any clue, I think the whole room is surrounded by several feet of this black material on all sides.

"And while this wall looks like black rock, it actually appears to be some form of gemstone; far harder than diamond. It really is fascinating stuff." He stood for a moment with his hands on his hips, smiling to himself.

"How is any of this relevant to-"

"Oh, right. Well, you see, I think something was trapped in here. In fact, I think it was this 'Siscci.'"

"You think the dwarves had a demon trapped down here for hundreds of years?"

"Well, it makes sense if you study the engravings. It's literally written on the wall, in so many hard-to-decipher words. Like this over here," he said, turning toward a wall. He walked over and pointed at the artwork, and the inscription underneath. "Now, you'll have to bear with me. Even dwarves don't speak ancient dwarven these days, so this is a little difficult to translate. This picture didn't make much sense to me before now, but after hearing your tale... I think it explains what has happened."

The engraving depicted several small humanoids, presumably dwarves, standing guard in front of a circle. Inside that circle was a single black figure with a white face.

"There are a few things of note about this one in particular. First, is that the dwarves drawn here represent women. Specifically, this is the way they draw older female soldiers. The males are usually drawn with a slightly more rotund waist, while the females are shown with a slightly more rotund upper torso. That is because their armor makes allowances for their differences in physiology. The fact that they aren't wearing helms, and have their hair on full display, indicates they are seasoned warriors, likely beyond birthing years.

"That may not seem significant unto itself, until accompanied with what you've witnessed. You say Siscci had no power to control you, or Aggie, or Jae. Both Aggie and Jae were beyond the age to bear children, and when that happens a woman's body goes through changes. You are before your years, and haven't yet entered the reproductive cycle. I... I think her power can only sway those within their reproductive prime; those with the proper physiological state to be swayed into desiring her."

"I'm sorry. I don't understand most of what you're saying, I'm afraid." She gave him a sheepish smile.

"What I mean is, her power of control only seems to affect those of the proper age to bear children. She can't affect children, or the elderly. I can confirm that from my own experience, because I was nearby when she broke free."

"You what?" She was more than a little upset that he hadn't mentioned that detail until that moment.

"As I said, I was down here studying the room. I left to go relieve myself at apparently the perfect time. There was a strange explosion, far above, that shook the mine. I started making my way back toward this room, fearing a collapse, and when I rounded the corner I saw this black figure from behind. It touched the two assistants I had cleaning the engravings on the walls, and climbed up through a fresh crack in the ceiling. The crack was sealed with rubble a few moments later, and I never saw it again.

"When I checked on my assistants, they were both decayed, like they'd been lying on the floor for over a decade. So, I dragged them into another room and covered them with blankets. Afterward, I found the door had been pushed open from the inside, and the empty room beyond.

"I searched the paths leading toward this chamber, and they were all caved in. My plan was to dig out through the tunnel with the straightest route to the surface. That's what I was doing when you found me."

"So I was correct in my assumption. Whatever Nightweaver did in Port Gandraias freed Siscci, whether she knew it or not. We found her there in the rubble, she took control of Johorr and Thomlin, and we brought her to Helmdale to feast and grow stronger." She suddenly felt like she was at fault for everything that was happening in Helmdale.

"Yes, it would appear so," he confirmed. "In fact, these drawings nearer the entrance depict the dwarves slaughtering whole villages and hunting something. I *think*—considering this new information—that they were killing everyone she'd infected, to weaken her and overtake her. As to how they got her into that prison? That doesn't seem to be on the wall. In this panel, they're hunting her down, and in the next they're guarding the chamber."

Jareth pointed at the various drawings as he was discussing them, then got lost in the strange text beneath the final one. He stood for a time, lost in thought, as he studied the wall. She thought about his words for a moment and then suddenly remembered the clothing she'd stolen from Siscci. In a moment of panic, she patted her chest, expecting it to be gone, only to discover the silken bundle was still safe and secure against her breast. She removed the pieces of silk from their hiding place and unfolded them. One by one, she lifted, shook and then laid them out.

Jareth joined her at the center of the room, and peered over her shoulder at what she was doing for a moment before inquiring. "Is this what she was wearing?"

"It is. I'm trying to figure out how to put it on."

"Why would you want to do that?"

"Well, it protected her. I watched as Jae attacked her several times with a dagger. None of the attacks found their target, and Jae was a very seasoned warrior," she explained.

"You think it's magical? That would be an amazing find!"

"I think it is, and I mean to use it to our advantage. After all, she's only a few inches taller than I am."

"Wait, you mean to go after her? It took an *entire army* of dwarves to defeat her before. What makes you think-"

"I *don't* think I can do it... but who else do we have? You said yourself it has to be someone very young, or very old. Not to mention, there's *nobody else* here to do it. We're the only ones that know what's going on. If we don't do something now—while she's still weak—her influence could spread across the land so far and fast that there wouldn't be anywhere left to hide! It probably took an army of dwarves because she had hundreds, maybe thousands, of those things under her command."

Sylk was getting used to being afraid. Ever since the strange event in camp the night before they met Nightweaver, she'd been living with one kind of fear or another. She'd tried to get away from Siscci twice, and both attempts had failed. What hope did she have of getting away on her third try, with them hunting for her? Siscci would know it unwise to let her get away. She wouldn't give up, and so Sylk couldn't either... afraid or not.

"You're just a child. What can you do against a... a... demon?" Jareth was beside himself. He couldn't comprehend what the small elven girl before him was thinking, let alone planning. All he wanted to do was get away from whatever creature was loose in Helmdale. "Look... My wife and daughter, Erissa and Nadyra, are in Belaigne. That's where I'm going when we get out of here. I have to make sure they're safe. Besides, I'm no warrior. I wave a quill, not a sword. And you... you're nothing but a sl-"

"A slave? Yes. I *am* a slave. I'm also eighty-six years old. Sure, by elven standards, I may be a child. But by human standards, I'm old enough to be your mother. I think it's time I own up to what I am, and take a stand. Am I trained in combat? No. But, I've killed two men since this started. I escaped that demon twice already, *and* stole her enchanted clothing.

"There's *no way* she expects me to come back and attack her. Besides, where else am I going to go? I have *nothing*! I don't have a family waiting for me, or a place to call home. What I *can* do, is make sure nobody else has to suffer the way Helmdale... the way *Thomlin* suffered." Determination and anger laced her every word. She'd never spoken with such conviction, and had to admit it felt rewarding to do so. *No longer will I be the slave girl cowering in a corner!*

"I may not live through this. In fact, I really don't expect that I will. This silken garb gives me a fighting chance, and that gives you and your family a shot at getting away. Where do you think she'll go next, if something doesn't stop her?"

"Belaigne," he answered. The reality of their situation finally struck him. Gone was the wonder of discovery. Gone was his desire to study the event and document it for posterity. "She could be headed there now!"

"She could, and that's why you're going to help me figure out how to properly wear this. Then we're digging out of here, and you're going to point me toward Helmdale and run for Belaigne as fast as you can. Hopefully Siscci is still feeding on the citizens of Helmdale, and I can catch her off guard."

"The only weapon you have is a dagger. How do you expect to-"

"A dagger is all I'll need. I've never used anything else. Besides, I can't expect to go toe-to-toe with her mindless slaves-"

"Husks," corrected Jareth.

"Husks?"

"That's what the Dwarven script calls her followers, or at least... that's how I translated it. Your description of what she does to them supports my theory. She drains them, converting them into empty husks, then fills them with a new soul, or part of her own essence, or whatever it is. That's why they behave differently. They don't have all the memories of that body's former... occupant."

"Well, I don't expect to survive in a face-to-face fight with her husks. I'll have to kill them before they see me, or surprise them like I did Thomlin. I don't see any other way."

"You could just come with me to Belaigne. We can go to the King; explain what's happening?" He barely knew the girl, but felt a sinking sensation in his gut at the thought of her throwing her life away.

"Do you really think a King is going to believe the story we have to tell? '*Hey, so, um... this ancient witch you tell bedtime stories about accidentally freed a demon that drains souls and takes people as mindless servants. She's kind of taking over the countryside right now, and, um... would you kindly find a bunch of elderly knights to go kick her butt for us?*' Yeah, no," she mocked.

"Well, when you put it like that..."

∴ ∴ ∴

THEY SPENT the next several hours studying the silken outfit, trying to figure out how it pieced together. After a bit of trial and error, they finally got everything to line up properly. Sylk stood beside a lantern so that Jareth could give it his final approval, and spun around slowly so that he could see from every angle.

"Well, you must be wearing it correctly," he stated. He squinted his eyes, trying to see more clearly.

"Why's that? Why are you squinting like that?"

"It's suddenly very hard to focus on your body. The only things I can see clearly are your face, hair, hands and feet. Everything else is just a touch off; blurry, like I need to wear a pair of spectacles. Although, knowing what I know about this outfit, I'm certain that wouldn't help."

"Then it's working!" She was excited to hear that something

was finally going as expected, rather than turning into a nightmare before her eyes. She decided to embrace that glimmer of hope, and ignore the impending sense of doom her subconscious insisted was appropriate for the task ahead.

"Yes. It appears you will, indeed, be harder to hit in a fight. However, I urge you to still attempt to dodge any incoming attacks. I doubt that layer of silk actually deflects blows that find their way through."

"Of course I'll dodge. But the plan is to not be seen, and fight only as a last resort."

"Then I think you've got a shot, at least until you face Siscci. You're very hard to see in the dark with that on, aside from your hair."

"Oh, right! Maybe I could rub ash in my hair from a campfire; blacken it a bit, and make it not so bright and reflective?"

"That could work. I... I have to admit, I would feel fairly uncomfortable encountering someone dressed like you in an alley, no matter how safe Lothenheim is."

"Alright, enough of this. That tunnel isn't going to dig itself out," she said.

"I'm still not sure I feel right with you trying to face this on your own." His forehead wrinkled with lines of worry. "Once I find my family, I'll send help."

"Right," she sighed. *By all means, send more victims for her to claim.* "Well, we can't do anything until we're out of here." She moved toward the chamber door and looked back, inviting him to follow. "Shall we?"

∴ ∴ ∴

SYLK SHOVED the last stone, sending it cascading down the pile of rubble to the stone floor on the other side of the cave-in. The clanking of stone on stone echoed through the mineshaft in all directions. It was a sound they'd grown accustomed to, but this time the opening they'd created and the empty shaft beyond amplified it.

"Do you think I can fit?" asked Jareth, standing on the floor behind her and nursing his bloody hands. He'd insisted on doing most of the heavy lifting throughout the day, and she was certain he was coming to regret that decision.

"I do. We should get moving. I-" she started, looking back over her shoulder at him. Her words stopped short when she heard movement in the newly exposed tunnel.

"You what?"

"Shhh!"

Jareth looked up at her with concern and listened intently. She leaned her right ear closer to the opening. The faint sound of footsteps echoing through the chamber, and the clattering of small pebbles became clear.

"Someone's coming," she whispered. Without waiting for Jareth to respond, she slid through the opening on her belly and disappeared into the dark shaft beyond. She crawled on her hands and feet, carefully selecting a path down the pile that seemed to have the most stable, larger stones.

Once she reached the bottom, she ducked into a small alcove at the side of the main hall. Ancient miners had placed wooden beams to create support for the opening of a new shaft, but they had never completed the tunnel. She backed into the corner and squatted down behind one of the beams to watch for whoever was coming. As she got into position, her right hand landed in a pile of loose dirt.

Taking her idea from before, she scooped up handfuls of the dirt and rubbed it into her hair. She completed her make-shift disguise just in time, and stopped moving abruptly as two men came into view.

The light of a makeshift torch danced playfully across the walls, illuminating the area a few feet around them. They seemed to be inspecting the walls as they moved, navigating their way through tunnels they were unfamiliar with, or searching for something.

"It came from just up ahead," said one.

"What makes you so sure?" said the other.

"Just trust me."

"You really think she'll reward me when we're done?"

"Why wouldn't she?"

"We've been waiting since the beginning."

"Patience, Davin. All in good time."

"Easy for you to say, you've already had your turn."

"I had to earn my place, as do you," said the man. They rounded the corner into full view of Sylk, and stopped in their tracks. "As I said," he continued, pointing at the opening in the pile of rubble.

"Someone's down here? I thought we were just... you know, destroying a chamber?" worried Davin.

"And now our mission has changed," said the other as he drew his dagger. "I wish I was ready to feed. Such a waste."

"I asked if we should bring rations. You said-" started Davin.

"Climb up. They must be hiding inside the chamber."

Sylk watched as the men slowly ascended the pile of rocks, knocking several stones loose in the process. She moved up behind them, using the sound of rocks shifting and falling as cover.

Davin reached the torch into the opening at the top of the rubble and leaned in behind it, looking for whoever might be on the other side. The other man leaned toward the opening, attempting to peer past Davin's head and shoulders.

Sylk slowly drew her dagger as she got into position behind their knees. She could feel a wave of cold wash over her as the anticipation of what she was about to do brought forth every ounce of anxiety her subconscious could muster. Choking back on the fear that quickly followed, she pushed herself into action. Using all her strength, she swung the dagger with her right hand toward the crease in the back of Davin's left knee.

The blade easily sliced through the man's simple cloth braes and the tendons beneath his flesh. He screamed in pain, instinctively attempted to stand, and bashed the back of his head into the top of the opening.

The other man twisted at the hip, and whipped around to face Sylk. She continued the motion in her arm, and reached up to drive the blade into the man's gut, which he'd just exposed to her with his change of position. She waited for the feeling of soft flesh giving way to her steel blade, then wrapped her other arm about his waist and leaned backward.

His shift in position had put him slightly off balance, making it easy for her to pull him the rest of the way down. Her maneuver was just enough to send him toppling over her head and down to the rocky floor below. She rolled on her heels, shifting her weight to act as a pivot point for his fall, and ended up landing on top of him.

There was a distinct crunch as the man slammed into the unyielding stone below, splitting the back of his head just enough to send his body into convulsions. Davin tumbled down the pile of rubble and landed next to him, screaming and holding the back of his leg. Sylk pulled herself free of the first man and retrieved her dagger. As she approached Davin, he began to plead for his life.

"No! Please," he said, holding a bloody hand up in a vain attempt to block her.

Davin rolled onto his rump and began sliding backward across the floor to get away from her, all the while pleading for his life. She couldn't let herself see him as a victim. He was serving Siscci, and longing to be converted. If she let him live, he'd turn her in the first chance he got, and she knew it. *I have no choice.*

Sylk grunted and walked toward him with the dagger in her right hand. To her, the grunt was the outward expression of willing herself to act despite her own fear and reservations. To Davin, the grunt sounded cold and filled with hate.

As the inky black figure approached, Davin lost control of his bladder and slowly grew paralyzed with fear. He'd spent the past few days dreaming of having his way with Siscci, and as far as he was concerned, her evil twin was about to kill him in cold blood... and there was nothing he could do to stop her. Air choked and sputtered in his throat as he attempted to breathe, despite the blade she was slowly pushing through it. She sat for a moment, straddling Davin's legs as the last of his life left his eyes, then pulled the dagger free and wiped it clean on his tunic.

"He never thought you capable," said a raspy voice behind her.

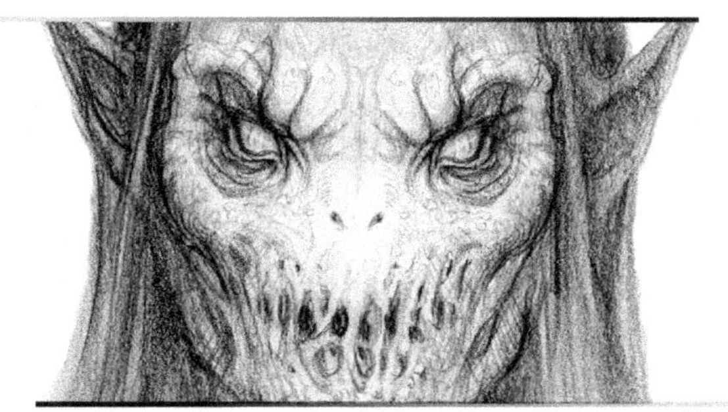

JOHORR

Ris'Uttyr, Amaethur 17th, 575 of the 1st Era

SYLK SPUN on her heel and stood. The creature before her seemed to be half human, half demon. Its skin was split and torn, as if the horrible beast within was slowly pushing its way through the flesh that contained it. What was emerging from underneath appeared similar to Siscci, yet lankier, with longer limbs and talons.

She didn't completely recognize the voice, but thought she sensed hints of the familiar in its tone and inflection. When she looked down and realized what the horrid being was wearing, the truth of its nature became obvious.

"Johorr!" she gasped.

"Imagine you being my first meal," said Johorr through his flesh-tethered lips. His vertical eyes narrowed into slits, and his nostrils flared. He approached her menacingly; hunched over with his talons spread wide, ready to strike. "This husk despised you. Such a long life, wasted in servitude... and you weren't even good for *that!*" it hissed. "Oh, to drink of an elf!"

The demon lunged for her, slashing at her chest with his right hand. Sylk jumped back, narrowly avoiding its attack and nearly tripping over Davin's corpse. She readied her dagger and slowly stepped to her right, skirting the edge of the pile of rubble.

"What's going on?" yelled Jareth. She could sense he was looking out through the pile of rubble, but couldn't risk the time to glance back and verify.

"Seal the hole! Hide!"

"Do you think I can't move a few stones?" cackled the demon.

It jumped toward her with a flurry of attacks. Each talon narrowly missed her twice before she could respond. She bent her knees as quickly as she could, setting her body into motion to leap backward out of the way. Before she could complete the maneuver, the creature backhanded her face and growled with rage. The force of the impact sent her sprawling. As she scrambled back to her feet, the demon roared its displeasure.

"Siscci's shroud is not meant for you! She... will reward me greatly for its return."

Sylk's heart was beating so fast it felt as if her chest was about to explode from the pressure; a feeling that was nearly drowned out by the searing pain in her jaw and pulled muscles in her neck.

The creature jumped toward her again, slashing with its talons in alternating strikes. She dodged as best she could, but nearly every blow missed by mere inches. The silk she wore was saving her life. She knew it, and the creature knew it. Her feeble attempts to deflect a few of the attacks with her dagger were quite telling; she had no business fighting the creature on her own.

I was right! I can't fight them face-to-face.

Sylk ran as fast as she could. The creature cackled in delight from behind, and it wasn't long before she could hear its footsteps chasing her. She did her best to run atop the small patches of dirt scattered along the tunnel, but those efforts were not enough to avoid the inevitable; running on uneven rocks and stone very quickly injured the soles of her feet.

Just what I needed, she lamented as the pain in her feet joined the myriad cries of muscle, tendon, and flesh across her body. *I have to find a place to hide so I can sneak up on it! Is that even possible?*

A dark passage opened up on her right as she passed under a partially fallen support beam. She ducked into the tunnel and quickly glanced around. Just ahead on her left was a small crack in the wall, just big enough for her to fit inside; nestled behind an old wooden beam. Without hesitation, she ran over and climbed in, then covered her head with the flowing silk hanging from her arms.

The demon scrambled into the tunnel and stopped a few paces inside; searching for her. He eased forward, one horrid step at a time, studying the darkness for signs of her passage. Every step put him closer to her hiding place, sending new waves of panic radiating through her core.

She shortened her breath involuntarily, and consciously fought back against the panic that was slowly threatening to cause her actual harm. The pain in her chest, and the labored nature of her breathing, sent her mind racing with all the possible ways she could die from the fear that welled up within her. *He doesn't need to catch me. If I can't calm myself down, my heart will do his job for him!*

Sylk closed her eyes and focused on her breathing. She latched onto the only repetitive sound she could hear, and tried to match her inhales and exhales to the beat. As the demon's left foot slapped down onto the stone just outside of her hiding place, her breathing finally fell into rhythm with his own.

She opened her eyes again, and carefully peaked between the crossed folds of silk she'd draped in front of her face. Johorr's waist was directly in front of her; inches away from the edges of the crack she'd crawled into. Tattered remnants of his clothing clung loosely to him, as if adhering to the acrid moisture that slowly seeped from his flesh. The skin that shone through the rips in the fabric was slowly shifting between dark brown, blood red and peach, as if pools of blood and feces slowly moved through his body just below the top layer of tissue.

Small pustules slowly formed, burst and faded in rapid succession all across his flesh. She was close enough to hear the sound of each one as it popped and sent puffs of horrid stench into the air. With her breathing and heartbeat finally under control, she found herself nearly overtaken by the urge to vomit.

Johorr turned and faced the wall she was hiding behind. As his hips twisted and feet jumped to their new position, her heart skipped a beat and her breathing stopped. She considered moving her hand toward the dagger, and preparing to strike him before he could notice, but her arm refused to comply with her request. She was paralyzed by fear, and there was nothing she could do to fight it.

He started bending at the hip, lowering himself down toward the hole in the wall. She could hear him sniffing wildly, the air rushing through the two slits serving as his nostrils in rapid, deep heaves. His claws slowly scraped the stone above the hole. Her breathing quickened again out of reflex, and she pushed back into the hole as far as she could. Several sharp edges on the wall behind her sent pain radiating through her back as they slowly dented and tore into her.

"Yes," he moaned in delight. "Your fear is delectable!"

Booted heels rounded the corner.

∴ ∴ ∴

JOHORR WHIPPED around to see the source of the noise. The boots stopped short—barely entering the tunnel—as if their owner suddenly regretted entering. "Leave her alo-" started Jareth's voice. Sylk could hear panic set in as he realized what he was looking at.

"Just what I needed," said the demon gleefully, "a snack before I dig the welp out of the wall!"

Jareth was able to take a single step back before he froze in terror. Urine stained his leg and pooled on the floor beside his left foot as the demon approached, cackling with joy at its fortune.

Sylk willed herself to move. She couldn't sit by and listen while Jareth—the man that had healed her wounds and put himself in harm's way to save her—fell victim to the unnatural creature Johorr had become.

She made it out of the wall in time to see the demon's horrific face hovering inches away from Jareth's. Her knees were weak from fear, but she managed to make her way toward the feeding beast's back without it noticing. Her right hand trembling, she retrieved the dagger she'd stowed on her belt and slowly raised it into position, point-first toward the base of the thing's skull.

Her breath caught in her throat as Jareth wheezed, nearing the end of his life. His cheeks sank in and shriveled slightly, fading to gray as if he were decaying before her eyes. She reached her left hand back behind her head. With all her strength, she drove the dagger into the demon's flesh with her right and pounded the weapon's pommel with the palm of her left.

There was an eerie squish as the metal blade slid into the skin and muscle, followed by a crunch and pop as the blade erupted through the creature's spine and exited its mouth on the other side. The strange energies transferring between Jareth and Johorr abruptly stopped as both of them crumpled to the ground, violently ripping the dagger's hilt from Sylk's grasp as they went.

∴ ∴ ∴

SYLK WEDGED her foot against the back of the demon's skull and pushed while pulling at the dagger's hilt with both hands. As the blade came free, Jareth quietly wheezed and attempted to reach for her from his prone position.

She dropped the blade. The sound of it clattering to the floor echoed through the chamber, drowning out the sound of the demon's own gasps. As she knelt beside Jareth, his eyes grew wide in panic; affixed on what lay behind her.

The demon's eyes blinked twice, and its flesh-tethered lips attempted to move, as if trying to speak.

In a panic, she retrieved the dagger from the floor and jumped on top of Johorr, pinning its immobile arms to the ground with her knees. Knowing the creature's spinal column had been severed, she decided to complete its decapitation from the front, and began sawing at the demon through the back of its mouth, just above the hinge in its jaw.

She thought of all the times Johorr had whipped them. Years of torment flooded her mind, fueling her rage and drowning out the sight before her. She didn't notice the sound of tearing flesh, or blade scraping against bone. All she could sense was the anger within her, and the need to end the creature's life once and for all.

Just as her arms were about to tire of the act, the creature's head popped free of its corpse with a final gush of puss and blood, and the dagger grated against the stone underneath. She stood up, exhausted, leaving the dagger behind, and kicked the head a few feet further down the hall.

Jareth attempted to reach for her again, but lacked the strength. He was fading fast, and as she looked down at the husk he'd become, she knew there was no way to save him. He'd given his life to save hers, and the only way she could think to return the favor was to seek out his family and make sure they were safe.

She knelt beside him again, and grabbed his feebly outstretched hand, cupping it between her own. The look in his eyes was not that of regret or panic, but of hope and thanks. He could see the determination in her face, and knew what she meant to do.

"I know how to defeat her now, thanks to you. She'll be vulnerable when she feeds. The hard part will be getting close to her. I just hope I can get there before more of them turn completely, like Johorr."

As the creature's rancid fluids slowly dried upon her hands, she held onto Jareth's for the final moments of his life. She was the last thing he saw of the living world, and she would be the last thing Siscci saw if she had anything to say about it.

Ris'Uttyr, Amaethur 17th, 575 of the 1st Era

DETERMINATION

Ris'Uttyr, Amaethur 17th, 575 of the 1st Era

YLK PULLED Jareth's boots off and sized them against her feet. Running across jagged stone had caused quite a bit of damage. She didn't want to risk walking through brush and dirt with her bleeding feet exposed. His boots were much larger than she needed, but she had no other options.

After a few moments of thought, she used the dagger to cut away strips of cloth from Jareth's shirt and pants, wrapped them in layers around her feet, and tied the strips into place around her ankles. With the extra padding, she'd be able to make the boots work for a short while. They'd make too much noise for sneaking through the city, but with any luck she'd make it to her destination without further damage to her feet, and hopefully the padding would help them stop bleeding.

After cleaning the dagger on the leftover remnants of Jareth's shirt, it dawned on her that the only part of her that would give her position away while sneaking was her hair. With a shrug, she leaned forward and began cutting her hair away.

Long, flowing locks of silky white hair drifted to the ground. The growing pile seemed reminiscent of fallen snow in the dark of the tunnel, easily reflecting the meager amount of light that managed to reach the area from the crevice above.

When she had cut away the majority of it, she used her left hand to guide the blade along her scalp. The sensation of the blade scraping her skin was both off-putting and soothing, all at once. The cool, damp air sent chills through her as it lighted upon her freshly exposed skin. It was a feeling she hadn't expected, and one she wasn't sure she disliked.

Her left hand glided over her freshly shorn scalp, revealing areas that had yet to be shaved or were in need of more attention. She managed to finish the task with only a few small nicks, and felt confident that she'd improved her stealthiness a great deal for the effort.

Content with her preparations, she stowed her dagger and jogged down the mining shaft in the direction from which the attackers had come.

∴ ∴ ∴

THE TUNNEL was longer than she expected, stretching for nearly a mile before it reached the surface. There were only a few bends in the main path, which eased her mind a great deal. She had no experience traversing underground passages. Getting lost would have been an abrupt end to her already treacherous quest.

Silence greeted her at the surface; a deathly calm that was quite unnatural for the wilderness. The day was overcast, and few beams of sunlight breached the clouds to reach the ground. All sense of time had evaporated. She didn't know how long she'd been underground, or whether the sun was rising or setting. Furthermore, she had no sense of where she was located. Had the exit to the mines been nearer to Helmdale or Belaigne? Was she somewhere in between them, or had she traveled past them? The cloud coverage above made getting her bearings nearly impossible, and with no sounds to indicate her proximity to civilization, she had no clues to work with.

She concentrated on her night vision, allowing her eyes to focus on the hidden spectrums that only elves could see clearly. Her eyes filled with the myriad shades of yellows, oranges and reds indicative of heat. Accompanying those hues were the more ethereal blues and purples cast off by the reflection of indirect, almost omnipresent sunlight.

The two forms of vision were not often used simultaneously. With concentration, she'd learned to focus on one at a time, or both, as she saw fit. Lying awake at night for decades while her owner snored a few feet away had afforded her plenty of time to practice, even if she'd never had a reason to leverage those abilities in the past.

She didn't know which side of her blood granted her which type of night vision. Perhaps if she'd grown up with Elven parents, she would have learned more about what she was capable of. She felt, deep down, that heat vision belonged to only part of what she was, and that the other style of night vision belonged to the rest. While she didn't truly understand her gifts, one thing she was certain of was that they would lead her out of the wood and closer to her target.

As she peered around, trying to gain her bearings, she noticed what seemed to be a bright ball of yellow, glowing in the distance through the trees to her left. She crept closer, taking care to place her feet down slowly and make as little noise as possible. Every movement seemed to echo off the trees in much greater volume than seemed reasonable.

Her heart was racing again.

After what seemed like an hour, she found herself near a clearing. The light on the other side was brighter than she could stand to look at, and seemed to dance and play, casting strange shadows about the ground around her. She closed her eyes for a moment and focused on seeing normal light once again. When she looked up, the entire city of Helmdale was burning before her; black smoke billowing into the sky like a massive, mile-wide chimney.

They left Helmdale and burned the city down behind them. Siscci must be on her way to Belaigne!

Sylk was certain the sky was less overcast than she originally surmised. What she'd thought to be clouds were the remnants of Helmdale blotting out the sun. She'd been so focused on seeing and hearing the world around her, she'd neglected to notice the stench of burning buildings and corpses in the air. It was a mistake she hoped she wouldn't repeat.

With her bearing gained, she reached down and pulled off the oversized boots. She knew where she was, and how to get where they were going. She only hoped she would arrive before it was too late to save Jareth's family.

. . . . .

SYLK RAN along the side of the road, heading north toward Belaigne. She decided to stick to the grass in order to protect her feet, reduce the noise she was making, and keep close to the trees in case she needed to make a hasty retreat. Long years of traveling barefoot had served well as preparation, but the wounds on her feet and the pain radiating up through her legs with each impact prevented her from running at full speed.

Several hours passed before she caught sight of anyone ahead of her. When she did, she immediately slowed down and ducked closer to the trees in hopes they wouldn't notice her approach. She followed them for hours, slowly gaining ground and constantly adjusting her speed to avoid overtaking them.

Siscci was standing on a small wooden platform suspended above the crowd on two long horizontal poles. Eight men walked at the center of the formation with one of the poles nestled into the crook of their neck and shoulder; four in front, and four in the rear. The demon was wearing what looked to be hastily modified bed sheets in place of her silken robes, and slowly turned her head back and forth, surveying her servants as they traveled.

Sylk gave the black silk cloth on her torso a wicked smile, thrilled at the thought of depriving Siscci of her disguise; nay, her armor.

The group's pace slowed dramatically, coming to a near stop at a bend in the road. A church steeple was barely visible from Sylk's perspective, poking into the afternoon sky from beyond the trees to the right. A dozen men broke away from the group and ran ahead. Sylk assumed they were entering town to both make sure the way was clear, and to announce Siscci's arrival to her new quarry.

A chill ran down Sylk's spine. She suddenly felt as if she was being watched. As quietly and quickly as she could, she lowered herself down into the tall grass at the side of the road and slowly moved toward the treeline. None of Siscci's followers were looking in her direction, as best as she could determine, and yet the feeling persisted.

Once she reached the trees, she raised up onto the balls of her feet into a squatted position behind one; ready to move at a moment's notice, but hoping that she wouldn't have to. No part of her wanted to flee through the underbrush on her already-wounded feet.

After a few minutes, the group started moving again, and the feeling went away. *Was that Siscci sensing me*, she wondered. Several of the men escorting the group stayed behind to guard the entrance to the town, as if answering her unspoken question. *Yes, she sensed me. This... should be interesting.*

∴ ∴ ∴

IT TOOK almost an hour for her to sneak close enough to see the situation properly and consider her options. Three men stood outside of town, each one at least a foot and a half taller than her. A frontal assault was out of the question, and attacking from the rear was impossible to accomplish silently with their height advantage. She simply wasn't confident she could properly reach their throats with her dagger without alerting the rest of them.

On top of the obvious risk of attacking them, she was keenly aware of just how hungry she was and how weak she'd become as a result. She hadn't eaten since Jareth's stash of bread, and wasn't used to going more than half a day without food; substantial food full of nutrients, at that. If nothing else, Johorr had kept them well fed. After all, a healthy slave could work harder.

Nothing in her immediate vicinity would serve as a meal, or even a reasonable snack. She'd left the mines in such a hurry, she'd neglected to grab any food to take with her. As she squatted behind yet another tree, the humor of her situation suddenly struck her; racing headlong toward a demon's army, without even bothering to bring food... dooming herself to lose the fight because she lacked the energy to overcome insurmountable odds.

I'll have to do better next time, she mused. *Next time? Am I expecting this to be a habit?* She rolled her eyes at herself, completely amazed at that line of thinking.

She turned toward the town and studied what she could see. A few homes, a general store, a church of Galrath, a small tavern; Belaigne was much smaller than Helmdale. However, while Helmdale seemed centralized around a large inn fit for travelers, Belaigne struck her as more of a holy destination, due to the unnecessarily large place-of-worship located at its heart.

Siscci's base of operations in Helmdale had been the inn. It was the largest building in town and offered plenty of room for her entranced followers. By that reasoning, Sylk assumed her base in Belaigne would be the church. If she was right, that would mean the general store or tavern would either be unguarded, or completely free from her people. If hunger was an issue, perhaps it was wise to solve that problem first.

She looked for possible routes that would take her to the general store without being seen. Very few buildings sat along the treeline, and those that did appeared to be mostly stables, outhouses and small sheds. Crossing the road directly would put her out in the open; something she did not desire.

The only way to the general store across the street was to go around. If she traveled through the woods to the far side of town, and then around behind the row of buildings back toward the store, there might be a chance. Rather than second-guess her decision, she moved as quickly as she could through the woods toward the east, while making as little noise as possible.

As she neared the rear of the first set of small buildings on her left, a door swung open a short distance away, rebounding off the wall beside it. She stopped in her tracks and eased back against the wooden outer wall of the outhouse she was next to. Two voices broke the silence as she brought her dagger up to her chest, and slowed her breathing to hear them more clearly. If they were coming to find her, she needed to know before they rounded the corner, and needed to be prepared to defend herself.

"I bet she chooses Harven next," said a man.

"Harven? That dolt? Why ya figure?" questioned a younger man.

Their feet scuffed the dirt road as they approached the building Sylk was hiding behind. Her heart started to race in anticipation.

"I figure she wants the strongest of us first, yeah?" suggested the first.

The door of the small building swung open with a creak, and Sylk could clearly hear the sound of a belt buckle being undone. Her anxiety instantly washed away and nearly caused her to sigh instinctively. She'd caught herself just in time.

"Ya think that matters to her? I mean... if'n so, I'll be dead last, right?"

"We'll all get our turn, lad. Don't worry 'bout it. I'm just sayin' not to get your hopes up too much. We got a line of folk ahead of us. Don't wanna go wastin' your load early," he laughed.

"I guess," answered the younger one as the outhouse door clanked shut.

"She's nuthin like anyone I've ever seen." The walls of the outhouse muffled the older man's voice, and the sounds of him relieving himself punctuated his words. The smell that followed was nearly instantaneous. "First she'll take us to the heavens, then we'll join her army and show those southern bastards what true strength is!"

"Yeah, but I thought we was headin' north first?" The younger man was pacing in front of the outhouse, kicking his feet into the dirt in frustration. The older man's bowels had not finished their job and seemed intent on disrupting their conversation.

"We'll go where she says to go, yeah?"

"I suppose," moaned the youngster.

Sylk could barely contain her distaste for the smells the man was producing, or the sounds of their creation. She decided that she needed to get away from the men, but wondered if they couldn't serve as a distraction for the rest. A quick glance at the outhouse's rear, and the small shed next to it, told her that she could easily climb on top. With a nod, she made her decision, picked up a twig, and got to her feet.

Snap!

The twig she broke echoed much louder than she'd expected. It was as if the whole world went silent just in time for her to make that one intentional noise. She'd hoped to draw the attention of the younger man, but felt a sudden panic that she might have alerted the entire town instead.

"What was that?" asked the older man, still doing his business.

"Dunno, pa." The younger man made his way to the side of the outhouse, squinting at the woods for the source of the noise. He hunched over and pushed his face forward, studying the darkness as best as his human eyes could. "Don't see anything."

Just as his head came into view, Sylk lunged toward his outstretched neck with her dagger. The move was swift and effective. The boy's body crashed to the ground almost instantly, his hands grasping frantically and pointlessly at the gaping wound in his throat. She turned and sheathed the dagger in one motion, then scaled the small shed as quickly as she could.

"James?" called the older man. She could hear his belt jostling about as he hurried to pull his pants back up. As he burst through the door, she pulled herself atop the outhouse and crawled toward the side where James lay dying.

The man rounded the corner and froze in his tracks, horrified at the sight of his son bleeding out in the underbrush. He looked around for a second, hoping to find the perpetrator, but his search was in vain.

Sylk pulled herself to the balls of her feet as he came into view. When his head whipped side to side in search of her, she jumped down from the outhouse and landed on his back. The force of her sudden impact threw the man off balance, crashing him to his knees with a violent jolt.

"Hel-" he began to yell, but his words were cut short by the sudden dagger in his throat.

She jumped off the man as he tumbled the rest of the way to the ground and ran as fast as she could south through the woods, with no care for stealth. After a few hundred feet, she stopped and turned back east toward the far end of town, and moved with greater care.

Her heart was racing and the panic inside her insisted she move quickly, but she knew she couldn't allow the enthralled to discover her ruse. She chose her steps carefully, preferring moss and other soft surfaces that wouldn't leave footprints. Her left hand was trembling from hunger, and her stomach was in knots. She wasn't sure how much longer she could push herself without eating. She had to get to the general store.

It didn't take long for cries of alarm to ring out behind her. When the sounds of people crashing through the underbrush began, she nearly panicked and ran. All she wanted to do was get away from the entire situation. Every instinct was telling her she was doomed. *I will not run and let this happen to city after city! Besides, I promised Jareth I would save his family.*

She pushed aside the fear as best she could and stayed the course, carefully choosing her steps and making calm, consistent progress toward the eastern edge of town. At least a dozen people were pursuing her through the wood, but thanks to her route and tactics, they were headed in the wrong direction. Confused voices, and arguments, rang out through the night as they reached the end of her hurried flight south, and her trail vanished.

Sylk couldn't help but smirk as she imagined the anger and confusion contorting their faces.

∴ ∴ ∴

THE HOMES along the eastern edge of the town square were dark and silent. On any given night at that time of year, one could have expected a wood stove or fireplace to be burning; sending puffs of smoke into the night sky. She found no such signs of comfort escaping the homes that night. Much like Helmdale before, the citizens of Belaigne had gathered near Siscci to await their conversion with lust clouding their every thought.

  Ris'Enliss, Amaethur 18th, 575 of the 1st Era

The general store is more likely to have dried meats and nuts that I can just eat, but one of these homes might also have something I can eat without cooking. They would certainly be the safer choice if they do, she decided. She needed food, but didn't have the time to stop and cook a full meal; to say nothing of the attention that would get her. However, she was no longer certain she could make it to the store safely, and her hunger was far more painful than she'd hoped.

She approached the back door of the first house and slowly tried the latch. It clicked as she depressed it, but the door wouldn't budge. *It must be barred from the other side.* Sylk moved back down the steps and toward the back of the neighboring home. As she drew closer, she could hear what sounded like weeping, and paused for a moment to study the sound.

"It's okay, Nadyra, they won't find us," said a woman with a strange accent, barely above a whisper.

The voice came from inside the second home, in the corner room near the window above Sylk's head. She snuck over to the wall and raised up on her tiptoes toward the window. It was too high for her to see in.

"Erissa?" whispered Sylk. There was no response, so she continued, "Jareth sent me to help."

"Jareth? Where is he?" answered Erissa a little too loudly.

"Let me in and I'll explain," whispered Sylk.

"Back door," answered Erissa.

"Who is it mom?" asked Nadyra.

If Erissa answered Nadyra, it was too quiet for Sylk to hear. She lowered herself back down and made her way to the back door and waited. After a few moments, the door slowly opened enough for Erissa to peer out. She took an involuntary step back at the sight of the black silk clad Dynar woman on the porch.

"It's okay, I'll explain everything," assured Sylk as she pushed her way through the door.

Once the entry was closed and secured, she turned back to Erissa with her hands held out to indicate she wasn't a threat.

"Where's Jareth?" blurted the woman.

"Keep it down. I heard you from outside, and that means they could as well. Let's move to the center of the house, not an exterior wall."

Erissa nodded and left to retrieve her daughter. Sylk carefully entered the main room of the home, half expecting that the scene could be a trap. Several plush chairs formed a ring around the fireplace, each made of ornate wood and exquisitely wrapped in fleece. Paintings hung from three of the walls, surrounded on all sides by small shelves holding tiny pieces of art. Whoever owned the home was quite wealthy, at least by any standard Sylk had ever experienced.

As she studied the room further, she noticed the faint smell of meat and vegetables coming from behind her. A pot was hanging from a crook over the cold ash and logs in the fireplace; remnants of the owner's pottage sat within, covered by a thin layer of solidified broth.

Without hesitation, she rushed over and knelt before the fireplace. When Erissa returned, she saw Sylk eating directly from the pot, her torso half submerged in the firebox, slurping ladle after ladle of day-old stew.

"I could make you something more appeti-" started Erissa, more than a little amused at the sight.

Nadyra giggled.

Sylk emerged from the fireplace, ladle still in hand and stew smeared across her cheeks and chin. She attempted to shush the pair, but the broth in her mouth spattered through her lips instead. Thankfully, the finger she placed in front of her mouth during the gesture was enough to let them know what she intended.

Erissa retrieved and presented a handkerchief, which Sylk gladly took and made use of. She then urged Jareth's family to take a seat on the floor near her, next to the fireplace. Nadyra wiped the remnants of tears from her cheeks with a grin and plopped down happily. Her mother sighed and joined her.

"I have some difficult news, I'm afraid," said Sylk.

Erissa's eyes immediately welled with tears. She shook her head and waved off Sylk's next statement, making it clear she didn't want Nadyra to hear the details. Sylk was slightly taken aback at the sight. Not because of how Erissa responded, but because it was the first time she'd noticed what the woman was. She'd been so intent on food and safety, she'd neglected to recognize that the woman was an Afyr.

She was a beautiful, adult, elven woman of indeterminable age. Thin and fairly frail in appearance, with pale skin and silvery hair. Her clothes spoke of humble wealth, but not enough wealth for the home to be hers. Nadyra, meanwhile, was dressed as any pauper's child; likely so that she could play with reckless abandon, without worry of damaging her more expensive clothing. The little girl was a halfling, and her human blood made her nearly as tall as Sylk, though she seemed no older than thirteen. Her black hair was quite striking when seen in contrast to her mother's.

"Your father won't be able to join us, Nadyra. He sent me in his place, to make sure you were both safe," said Sylk.

"Did he send you from Lothenheim? He works with a Dynar in Lothenheim named Badris. Are you Badris's daughter?"

"I'm afraid not, no. I am only half Dynar. The rest of me is Afyr, like your mother."

"Oh, neat! I never considered half elves could be half of two elves!"

Sylk stifled a laugh and lowered her eyes directly in front of Nadyra's. "We come in all shapes and sizes, and we're all just as important as the rest. Never let anyone tell you otherwise."

"Do you know what's going on?" asked Erissa, indicating the town outside with a wave of her hand.

"Yes," said Sylk. She sat upright and considered for a moment how to phrase her words to inform Erissa without upsetting Nadyra. "A few nights ago a tragedy befell Port Gandraias, and freed a... woman named Siscci. She has the power to enthrall people, and over time she uses that power to seduce and... change them. Forever. When she's done, they become her servants and the person they once were is gone. Her influence affects a wide area around her. So, I assume Nadyra's birth was... your final-"

"Yes. She was a whole birth; born inside the womb. I cannot bear further children," answered Erissa nodding.

"While I'm sure that was hard for you and Jareth, it has saved your life. Siscci can only force her influence over those who are fertile."

"Oh?"

"Jareth showed me ancient dwarven script that was etched into a tomb. It said they guarded her prison with only elder, female guards. I am not yet of childbearing age, and am not affected. Two other women I met were beyond their years, and were not affected. This confirmed to us that she cannot enthrall those who are incapable of reproducing."

"Ancient dwarves guarded Siscci? How old is she?"

"It's less about how old she is, and more about *what* she is. Siscci is some kind of demon. She wears a pearl mask to hide her true face, and uses her powers to make you see whatever you sexually desire. Some see a blonde woman, others a brunette. To some she might even appear as a man.

"This silken garb I wear was hers, and I believe she had greater influence while wearing it. It also protected her from harm. She took it off a few nights ago and used her magic to repair it. I grabbed it and fled when the woman I was captive with caused a distraction.

"That's when I found Jareth in the mines. He nursed me back to health, and we dug our way out of a collapsed tunnel. Then we were attacked. I defended us as best I could, but I wasn't strong enough to save his life. I'm... I'm sorry, I failed you."

Nadyra's eyes went wide during the story. When Sylk reached the end, her sense of awe shifted to sadness. It took every ounce of her self-control to keep from wailing over the loss. Instead, she quietly wept, with one hand firmly gripping her mother's thigh.

"It's okay," said Erissa, her eyes once again filling with tears. "You're but a child, and couldn't possibly have been trained to fight such a thing."

"She's not going to stop with Belaigne. She's going to take one village at a time, growing her army until she can conquer the entire Kingdom... possibly the world. I can't let her do that."

"But-"

"I know, I'm 'just a child'. I'm also a slave. Half Dynar, half Afyr, and welcome nowhere. I was raised by humans on a farm, and sold to a traveling merchant for drinking money. I have no family, no home, nothing. But that is how things will stay forever if I don't solve this now. If I do nothing, I'll never have a chance to be *anything*. If I want a life of my own, I have to make it happen... and that means taking a stand now. Or... there won't be anywhere *left* to make that life."

"That was the life facing me and Nadyra until Jareth stepped in. I... I left Vey'Thugohn to meet with a noble in Uldenheim for my father, and on the return trip we were beset by raiders from one of the human fiefdoms. They killed my guard, stole all our goods, then..." she paused for a moment and looked at her daughter. She'd never openly discussed the event in front of her. With much regret, she put her hand on Nadyra's and continued, "They... they raped me and left me for dead.

"When I returned home, my father banished me; said I was '*impure*' and not fit to live among the Afyr. I traveled north to Tellrindos hoping to find a better life, but I didn't have the skills to find employment with any of the trade folk I met. By the time I reached Lothenheim, I was near death and I was getting sick every morning. That's when I discovered I was pregnant.

"I tried getting help from the church, but they turned me away. I wasn't human, and didn't serve Galrath, so I was beneath them. I had no other options, so I slept on the street nearby. The building I took shelter beside happened to be the Eldenhall; the college of higher learning in Lothenheim. Jareth had an office there. He saw me the next morning on his way into the building and took pity on me.

"Once he learned my story, and discovered my... *condition*, he took me in and offered to marry me. Before long we were in love, and we've raised Nadyra like she was his own. I've... never talked about it in front of her. My biggest fear in all this was that we would lose Jareth—or that she would lose both of us—and she'd be left to survive on her own.

"For all their talk of being superior to the warring people of the south, Tellrindosians are a spiteful and judgmental people. They claim to care for the weak, but that is a fallacy. At most it is done for show; to gain praise from others. Jareth wasn't like the rest. He legitimately cared for us. He-"

Erissa's voice caught in her throat as she began to weep. Sylk lifted her haunch off the ground and shuffled over next to her. She wrapped the woman in her arms and pulled her into her shoulder, rubbing her back. Nadyra joined them, and gently kissed her mother's forehead.

Through all the years, Sylk had always thought of her life as being terrible, and never once wished to find anyone who'd gone through similar turmoil. Erissa had been through far worse, as far as she was concerned. Sure, she'd been beaten within an inch of her life on several occasions, but thankfully, she'd never been taken advantage of in such a way.

"I will get you both out of here. But to do that, I need to make sure Siscci can't follow us. We won't be safe until she's gone. Jareth gave his life to save mine, and in the doing taught me how to kill the demons she creates, and hopefully her as well. Now that I know you're both safe, I can see to the next part of my mission, and end her threat forever.

"What I need from you is to hide yourselves somewhere that you won't be found. They're out there looking for me right now, and it's only a matter of time before they check this house. If there's an attic or a crawl space, get there now and stay until I come to find you. If I'm not talking like myself, stay hidden until Siscci leaves, for it means I've been overtaken by her powers."

Siscci

"Are you sure there's nothing I can do to help?" wept Erissa.

"Hide so that I don't have to worry about you. That will be help enough," said Sylk.

CONFRONTATION

SYLK GAVE Nadyra and Erissa hugs before leaving. It was hard to be reassuring with what lay ahead, but she did her best to calm them both and put them at ease. With one last reminder to hide and stay hidden, she left the same way she'd entered.

From the quiet of the backyard she could hear what sounded like footsteps a few dozen yards into the woods to the east, and hushed chattering in the town square on the other side of the home. She knew from the dwarven script that killing the enthralled would weaken Siscci, or at the very least reduce the number of those protecting her. Killing the men that hunted her would have to be part of her plan.

She snuck into the woods, following the sound of crunching leaves and rustling underbrush. Before long, she caught sight of two men several yards apart from one another. They were walking north, scanning their surroundings for signs of whoever had killed the men at the outhouse. The one closest to her seemed frustrated.

"Whoever they are, they're long gone!" yelled the closer man. He fidgeted with a small twig in his hands as he spoke, paying far less attention to the task than his companion.

"If it's that elf wench from Helmdale, we can't stop looking. She wants her things back," answered the other.

"I'm going to miss my turn, damnit!"

"Your turn? It doesn't work like that. You go when you're chosen, and not before. It's not like there's some line forming and you lose your spot."

"There *is* a line, and you know it!"

"And she walked right past that line to pick Jonah, didn't she?"

"I guess," admitted the closer man.

Sylk snuck closer to the man nearest her position, using their conversation to help cover her footfalls.

"Just keep looking. If she wants you, she'll find you." The farther man turned east and knelt down, studying the underbrush.

"Find something?" asked the closer man, intrigued by the possibility of a clue, and the chance to end their search sooner rather than later.

"Nah, just some deer tracks," answered the farther man as Sylk arrived at the closest.

"See, this is pointle-"

The man's words stopped suddenly as Sylk's dagger entered his airway. Adrenaline rushed through her as she withdrew the blade. As he fell to the ground, she ducked between the trees behind him and crept a short distance to hide.

The other man ran over. He was much taller than the first, and far more muscular. "Oh, son of a!" He frantically searched the area, whipping his head in all directions. "I'll find you, bitch!"

Sylk studied the area and selected a path, then rose onto the balls of her feet, ready to move. "Harven, I presume?" Her taunt issued, she bolted to her new hiding spot and prepared for his arrival.

Harven turned toward the source of the voice and went into a jog. He came to a stop beside the tree she'd been behind and looked around. Using heat vision from her new vantage point, his face seemed to glow red with hatred. "If you know my name, you must know this won't end well for you. Best come out and get this over with. If I have to find you, it's going to be *so much* worse!"

She picked a new hiding place, and a path to it, then taunted the man again. "Oh, I doubt that very much." Once again, she went into motion just as her words finished, arriving at her new hiding place before he reached her previous position.

"Are you that afraid of an unarmed man?" he yelled.

Sylk climbed seven feet up the tree she was next to and wedged herself between the branches so that she could lower her torso and hang from her thighs at a moment's notice. For the second time since her haphazard adventure began, she found herself happy to have played in the trees with Samuel as a child. Once she was in position, she called out again.

"Afraid of a man who can't catch a small elven wench? I think not." In truth, her heart was racing and her palms were beginning to sweat. It was a strange sensation for such a cold night, and told her all she needed to know about just how bad her anxiety had become. As the situation progressed, however, she found her fear was slowly giving way to adrenaline. *Am I starting to enjoy this?*

Harven ran under the tree, just as she'd hoped. Her ruse had worked.

"Fuckin' *bitch*," he muttered under his breath. "You can't hide all night!" he yelled.

She tensed her legs and slowly lowered herself into position behind his head. He backed up a step—as if on queue—placing his ear shockingly close to her mouth. She reached around carefully, getting the dagger into position, and then whispered, "I don't have to."

Before he could respond, her right hand dragged the dagger across the front of his neck while her left palm pressed his back forward, all in one motion. Harven stumbled forward and turned to face her, shock and horror depriving his face of color. His left hand instinctively went to his throat, and his right slowly reached for her.

She slashed at his outstretched arm, hitting his hand and severing two fingers. He fell to his knees, his eyes still locked on hers. After a few seconds of gurgling and gasping, he fell to the ground sideways and expired.

Sylk lifted her torso back toward the branches, switched her grip to her hands, slid her legs free and dropped to the ground. She listened for a moment, but didn't hear anyone else coming. Without further delay, she ran the long way around toward the back of the church.

∴ ∴ ∴

THE VILLAGE was eerily quiet when she returned. She came in from the north, having circled around through the forest. Gone were the men she'd heard on the road. She couldn't see any sign of guards at the far end of town through the gaps in the buildings, and there was no indication of anyone wandering the woods in search of her.

The scene struck her immediately and sent a shiver down her spine. On the one hand, she had to assume Siscci knew she was coming and that the setting before her was a trap. On the other hand, she didn't have another course of action. Her only other option was to try and flee, and she'd be running for the rest of her life; to say nothing of the fate of Erissa and Nadyra.

She crept toward the rear of the church, half expecting armed men to round either corner at any second. She'd made it halfway to the building before she realized that there was no sound at all. No birds. No insects. No animals moving through the brush behind her. Not even her own footsteps, of which she'd learned to be keenly aware.

Panicked, she ducked and rolled... just in time. A blackened fist cut through the air just over her head as she moved; missing her by so little she'd felt the wind from its motion.

She came to a rest on the balls of her feet and spun to see one of Siscci's demons barreling down on her. The next few seconds were a blur as she haphazardly dodged left and right, attempting to avoid the creature's blows while she backed away; all the while slashing at it with her dagger.

Her back hit the church, its stone wall digging into her shoulder blades slightly with the force of her impact. She rolled right and whipped her dagger out toward her opponent mid-roll. His right fist slammed into the wall where her head had been, cracking the mortar that held it in place and rupturing the skin on its knuckles. Her dagger caught the left of the creature's chest on its way past, slicing open its brown-black, shifting flesh and spilling a dark black, blood-like ooze.

She couldn't hear it make the sound, but the fluttering of the flesh that stretched in strips between the demon's lips told her it was hissing. Its eyes narrowed as it hastened its attacks, sure of its victory. She started backpedaling again as fast as her body would allow. All her subconscious wanted to do was flee, but her body couldn't comply fast enough. As she dodged another fatal blow so narrowly she could have kissed the beast's fist, she considered the clothing she was wearing. *Isn't it supposed to defend me? Why isn't it helping? Or... is it helping?*

She focused her mind on dodging and defense, forcing her subconscious to focus just as she usually did when in a meditative state. As the two halves of her mind reached cohesion, the silk shimmered and began dancing about her, rippling in waves of elusive silk. Her body became a blur of motion, just as her energy waned and she found herself unable to do much more than stand still.

The creature lashed out at her repeatedly, its fleshy lip-tethers fluttering as it silently hissed in delight at the easy prey before it. Every attack hit precisely where the creature *thought* she was standing, yet missed her entirely. Enraged, it stepped forward and attempted to wrap her in its arms. She ducked under his grasp with ease and slid to the side.

With one calm thrust, she buried the dagger quillon-deep in the demon's left side, then twisted. The dagger wedged between the creature's ribs, leaving a gaping hole and allowing its lung to collapse and fill with blood.

The demon backed away from her with what she could only assume was horror painted across its terrible facade. It clutched the dagger frantically and pried the weapon free, cracking its ribs in the process. It attempted to hiss at her, but couldn't force the air past its lips. In desperation, it dropped the dagger and turned to flee back to its master.

She jumped forward, grabbed the dagger, and easily caught up with the stumbling, half dead demon. The first sound she heard throughout the entire encounter was the sucking sound as her dagger pulled free of the acrid flesh of the demon's right side, puncturing its other lung.

Remembering that Johorr was starting to heal a mortal wound to his neck before she severed his head, she briefly considered spending the time to decapitate the one lying beneath her. *I don't have that kind of time*, she decided. *Hopefully this is enough*, she thought as she drove the dagger into the creature's eyes, and into its brain; twirling it as best she could with each thrust to scramble the innards.

She drove the dagger into the ground to clean most of the black ooze and brain off before returning to the church.

.· .· .·

THE BACK door of the church opened silently. She half expected it to be locked, and was surprised to find that it wasn't. Low, repetitive chanting reached her ears as she stepped inside. The main chapel lay at the other end of the short hall she was standing in, and from her vantage point, she could see what seemed like all of Helmdale and Belaigne kneeling and swaying gently from side to side in a trance.

She crept to the end of the hall and crouched behind the edge of a small bookshelf. There were too many people to count at a glance, and all of them were chanting one name under their breath in unison, "Siscci."

The hall opened into a small room that was sunken halfway below the main hall, with only a half wall separating it from the congregation. At the far edges of the room were thin stairs leading up to the main level, right next to the curved stairs that lead up to the stage. The room was full of crates, shelves, extra chairs, and various assorted supplies the church might use during normal operation.

Sylk slipped into the room and hid behind a stack of lanterns and crates to get a closer look at the crowd. There was no immediate sign of her quarry anywhere in the crowd. Following the eyes of the swaying, enthralled masses she assumed that the demon was above her.

This isn't going to be easy.

Just as the thought processed in her mind, the front door of the church burst open and two men entered. They dragged someone who was kicking and trying to break free. Someone with silvery white hair.

Erissa! No!

The familiar feeling of panic and fear surged back into her. Every fiber of her being insisted she needed to do something. She watched in horror as another pair of men entered, dragging a small girl who was screaming and crying for her, "Mom!"

They stopped at the base of the stairs on Sylk's left. She slipped closer and hid behind a small desk that was stowed nearby. A man holding each of the captives put a hand over their mouths to silence them.

"We've brought you the last of them," said one of them. After a moment he seemed to answer an unspoken question. "No, there was no sign of her. But there's something else... Harven and Lukas never returned, and we found Golan dead out back." He paused for another moment, then responded again, "Yes, he was stabbed through both sides of his chest and his eyes. I'm sure she did it, but–"

He stopped mid-sentence as if being interrupted, and then

continued, "Are you sure? That's going to make you pretty weak, isn't it?" After a brief pause, he clarified, "I didn't mean anything by it. I've just noticed that when you... understood. We'll bar the doors."

One of the men raced toward the front door, and the other rushed past Sylk's hiding place to secure the rear door. As the bars dropped into place, Siscci's feet came into view, descending the stairs. Once she reached the bottom, she walked up to Erissa and gently stroked the woman's chin with the back of one hand. Her other hand removed the featureless white mask, and Erissa's eyes went wide in horror.

As the man who barred the rear door walked confidently past Sylk, Erissa's life essence streamed out of her and into Siscci. Nadyra screamed through her captor's hand. The swaying throng raised their palms toward the demon, and their chanting increased in volume.

A knot formed in Sylk's throat. She swallowed hard and slowly wiped the tears from her own cheeks. Her subconscious flooded with thoughts of Thomlin, Aggie, Jae, and Jareth. Everyone she cared about or who had tried to help her was dead because of the demon in front of her. And now, surrounded by dozens of mindless servants, she was powerless to prevent the death of a woman she'd sworn to protect.

Or am I?

.·. .·. .·.

SYLK LOOKED back at the crates and lamps she'd hidden behind a few moments prior. The lanterns were of the same style Johorr owned, and according to the symbol painted on the side of the crates, they were full of jars of lamp oil.

With no time to delay, she raced over to the pile. The first two lanterns she picked up were too light, and therefore empty. The third was heavy enough to have fuel in it, and directly beside it was an open crate that contained two bottles of oil. A fresh dose of adrenaline coursed through her in anticipation.

She removed the glass covering from the lantern and turned the key. Tiny sparks issued up from little gears and kissed the wick, setting it ablaze. She turned the wheel at the front, extending the wick higher, then set the lantern down momentarily. As quickly as she could, she uncorked one of the bottles of oil and then grabbed the lantern again.

With both in hand, she ran toward the stairs and willed her silken garb to defend her like she'd done outside. Siscci stopped feeding and spun away from Erissa at the sound of hastened footsteps approaching from behind. The jar of oil shattered violently at her feet just as Sylk reached the top of the stairs, followed closely by the blazing lantern.

The two men on either side of the small set of steps tried desperately to reach for Sylk and stop her, but their hands couldn't find purchase amid the blur of silk. Siscci screamed in horrific agony; the sound of a thousand voices escaping her all at once. She dropped the mask and tried desperately to snuff the flames that danced upon her acrid flesh.

Still running, Sylk scooped up the mask and tucked it into her top. She proceeded toward the men holding Erissa and stabbed them both in the bicep as quickly as she could, to force them to release their captive.

They dropped the elf, but immediately swung the fists of their uninjured arms in retaliation. She ducked under both and stabbed the one on her right in the groin. As she pulled the dagger free, the man wailed and fell backward. She turned to stand and attack the other, when a fist crashed full force into the back of her head and sent her toppling into his knees.

She nearly lost her grip on the conscious world but managed to land and roll to her left, through the legs of her intended target. He fell over her, his momentum sending his nose directly into the knee of the wounded man, who was rolling back and forth holding his crotch.

One of the new arrivals reached for her neck. She managed to slash at his arm in self defense, slicing through the tendons under his wrist. He backed away instinctively, bouncing into the second man that had approached her from behind. The disarray gave her just enough time to pull herself out from under the man who'd fallen over her as he attempted to stand.

As she gained her feet, she dragged the dagger across the fallen man's throat, and then brought it up into a defensive position between herself and the other two men. She forced her mind into a near-meditative state—like she'd done against the demon outside—and focused on defense. The silk flowed more feverishly, blurring her position in their view.

The men charged at her, jumping over their friends and swinging wildly. She backed away and swung the dagger toward their arms as best she could, leaving small cuts and gashes along their forearms.

Over their shoulders, Sylk could see Siscci moving up the stairs to the stage, her skin half burned away and smoldering. She reached her hands out toward the still-praying throng and began to chant in her demonic tongue.

Sylk focused her attention back on the men and doubled her efforts to wound them and drive them back. As the man on her left punched toward her face, she stepped past his attack into his reach, and drove her dagger into his underarm, burying it deep into his flesh. He screamed as best he could and stumbled back, tripping over his fallen comrades and landing head first in the fire that was quickly spreading behind them.

The second man spun to face her as she performed the maneuver and managed to drive his left fist squarely into her jaw, sending her sprawling across the ground toward the praying masses.

"Mom?" yelled Nadyra as she woke.

Sylk shook her head out of reflex and clamored to her knees. She looked up to see the man walking toward her. The dagger was still in her previous victim, and she had no way to retrieve it in time. Her mind raced, trying to find a way out of the mess that she'd created. Just before he reached her, an idea popped into her mind. She reached into her top as quickly as she could, grabbed the pearlescent mask and held it to her face.

∴ ∴ ∴

THE COOL, bone-like surface of the largely featureless mask pressed against her skin and seemed to latch on. There was a sucking sensation across her face and forehead, as if the back of the mask were coated in some form of adhesive that only engaged when it was worn. A chill ran through her body, washing down from her face to her feet. She felt instantly out of place, like she was disconnected from reality. She could see through the mask and breathe, despite the lack of holes with which to do so. It was a surreal experience; an amplified version of what she'd felt while in the throes of depression as Johorr's slave, before Thomlin came along.

The attacker backed away holding his right temple, as if he were suddenly confused. Assuming the mask might function in much the same manner as the magical silk outfit, she focused her mind into a meditative state and willed the man to see her as if she were Siscci. Slowly he backed away and a look of terror washed over his face.

"I'm... I'm sorry. I thought you were-" he began. His words

caught in his throat as she took a step toward him, confirming that the illusion had taken full effect.

The throng moaned in unison as the real Siscci began drawing their lives all at once from atop the stairs. Sylk pointed toward her, indicating to the man that he should go and stop her. He looked at her in confusion, and then toward the stairs. When he saw Siscci for what she really was, his face went white as a sheet and his eyes spread wide in panic.

"Kill!" demanded Sylk.

"I... I... where did that thing come from? You... you said you were here to protect us from a coming evil... is this... is this it?" he whimpered.

"Kill!" she repeated.

The man took no notice of the fact that Sylk verbally spoke her command. He was so accustomed to hearing Siscci's voice in his head, and seeing an unmoving mask before him, that he simply accepted the situation for what his eyes told him it was. After a moment of hesitation, he took a careful step toward his friend's corpse, retrieved the dagger, and started making his way around the fire.

Sylk reached down and helped Nadyra to her feet. The girl panicked at the sight of the mask.

"Shh. It's me," said Sylk. "Go to the front door and wait."

Nadyra nodded and ran to the door. Sylk turned her attention to Erissa and began slowly pulling the elf out from under the small pile of dead and dying men. Once her arms were out from under the pile, Sylk looped her hands under the woman's arms and tugged harder.

The man with the dagger jumped over the last stretch of flames and approached Siscci. He swung his arm back in preparation for a strike, and as it reached its peak, the demon broke free of her trance and grabbed him. She snapped his neck like he was nothing more than an inconvenience and tossed him aside. His corpse tumbled back down the stairs, and the dagger skipped across the ground, coming to rest next to the pile of bodies.

When Erissa was finally free of the pile, Sylk dragged her toward the door and laid her down gently next to Nadyra. She patted the young girl on the shoulder reassuringly and said, "Watch her, I'll be back."

Nadyra nodded again and sank to her knees beside her mother, crying.

Sylk walked back to the discarded weapon and picked it up. The demon's muscles and skin were beginning to grow back as she watched. That now-familiar sense of dread and fear crept back in, threatening to overtake the adrenaline that was keeping her going.

"You want their lives?" barked Sylk. "Better take them fast!"

With that, she ran into the crowd and started slicing open the necks of the enthralled, one by one. Half a dozen men and women fell under her blade while the demon screeched in disagreement. Siscci jumped toward her, bounding over the railing and the first few rows of mindless worshipers.

Sylk turned to face her. She walked sideways, stepping between the kneeling citizens and keeping at least one between herself and the demon at all times. The demon growled and spread its talons wide, ready to strike.

"This goes no further," said Sylk.

"You... cannot... win..." snarled the demon, forcing itself to speak her tongue.

"Can't I?" said Sylk as she casually split another throat with her dagger and stepped behind another worshiper. "What *are you* without them to feed you?"

"You wish to save them? And yet, you kill them," Siscci hissed.

"I wish to stop you, no matter the cost!" said Sylk as she slit another neck and moved further into the crowd.

Siscci screamed in anger and leaped toward the elf. Sylk ducked and shoved one of the enthralled into Siscci's path; her talons ripped the mindless victim's torso open like so much paper.

"I will just... start again!" insisted the demon.

"Not if I can help it." Sylk sliced another throat and jumped out of the way as Siscci leaped toward her again.

The demon stopped and backed up. She started chanting under her breath in her native tongue, and raised her hands slowly toward the ceiling. A chill washed over the room as strange energies flowed out of her.

The mindless thralls stood up.

.·.·.

SYLK DUCKED and dodged as the crowd turned toward her and started grabbing for her. She weaved her way through the crowd, trying to keep an eye on the demon and avoid her own capture at the same time. As the opportunity presented itself, she stabbed worshipers in the chest, throat, or groin. With each fatal wound, Siscci growled, hissed, stomped or lunged for her.

The macabre dance continued for several minutes until Sylk found herself standing with her back to the corner atop a pile of corpses, exhausted and desperate. More than half of the slowly shambling thralls were deceased or dying, but the rest were slowly making their way to her. Siscci was cackling to herself back atop the stairs as life energy streamed out of the crowd and into herself. The fire at the far side of the building was raging uncontrollably. The smell of burning bodies was filling the room, and the smoke was starting to hamper her ability to breathe and see.

Remembering the other jars of lamp oil, Sylk ran as fast as she could for the storage room. She scrambled across the unexpectedly soft bodies of the fallen and narrowly dodged two of the shambling worshipers on her way. As she neared the opening, she dove through the half-wall gap into the space beneath the stage, crashing into crates and bags as she landed. The landing hurt far more than she'd hoped, but she didn't have time to be in pain.

She grabbed the other bottle of oil she'd found earlier, uncorked it and poured a small stream behind her as she walked toward the set of stairs that was not yet ablaze. When she reached it, she cut her way through the thralls into the open room beyond, then threw the jar at the floor between the shambling horde and the open flames.

The liquid splashed onto nearby worshipers and coated the floor. The fire jumped to the liquid and quickly spread to the crowd as they turned to chase Sylk across the room. Siscci growled her displeasure as the flames danced across the front of the stage, igniting the railing.

Sylk bolted for the front door. Once there, she lifted the bar out of the way and pushed the door open, tossing the bar outside. She helped Nadyra pull Erissa out, and then shut the door as fast as she could; just as Siscci was arriving at it.

She wedged the bar under the door latch as best she could, but it wasn't enough to stop the flaming demon from bursting through, shattering a good portion of the door in the process. Sylk landed face first on the dirt and gravel road, sliding several feet before coming to a stop. She rolled over just in time to see Siscci land over top of her, straddling her legs, as shards of wood skittered across the ground.

Siscci

Ris'Enliss, Amaethur 18th, 575 of the 1st Era

SISCCI

Ris'Enliss, Amaethur 18th, 575 of the 1st Era

NADYRA SCREAMED from a few feet away. She leaned back against the church, holding her mother's head in her lap, trying her best to catch her breath and avoid passing out.

The demon roared and reached for the mask still affixed to the dark elf's face. Sylk drove her dagger up into the demon's outstretched wrist and twisted until the metal wedged between its bones. Black blood spurted out of the wound, spattering the pearlescent mask as Siscci reared back, wailing in pain.

Sylk took advantage of the opportunity and slid out from under the horrid creature. She got to her feet and looked around for a weapon; any weapon, or anything she could *use* as a weapon.

Siscci yanked the dagger free. The sound it made as it sucked free of her flesh and scraped the bones in her forearm made the tiny hairs on the back of Sylk's neck stand up. The demon tossed the dagger aside and approached its elven foe menacingly. Flames still danced upon its shoulders, upper arms, and head. Her hair had completely burned away. The stench of burning demonic flesh was nearly enough to make Sylk vomit. She was certain that in normal circumstances, it would have.

"Mom! Get up!" shouted Nadyra, gently patting her mother's face. "We have to go!"

Sylk jumped back as the demon unleashed a flurry of attacks, each one closer than the previous. The magical silk was protecting her, but she didn't know how long that would last against the demon that created it. She continued backing away, dodging attacks when she thought they might connect, until her heel bumped against something solid behind her.

Risking a moment to look back, she noticed a shard of wood from the door. It was heavily splintered, but sturdy enough on one end to grab with two hands. She stepped over it and ducked down quickly to take hold of her makeshift weapon, just as two more claw attacks whizzed past her head.

"Mom! Please!" begged Nadyra, her voice wavering. Several tears plopped onto Erissa's forehead and cheek. Her daughter frantically wiped them away, as if their presence somehow confirmed that she was doomed.

Sylk attempted in vain to parry the demon's volley with the shard of door. The very first attack hit the wood so hard it easily jarred the make-shift weapon free of her grasp and sent it flying. The second attack missed her chest by inches, and the third glanced ever-so-slightly off her mask.

Siscci was growing more furious with each attack. Her flesh was no longer burning, but thin beads of steam were still wafting skyward from the remnants of her charred skin.

Erissa's eyes opened. She looked up at Nadyra with more pain in her eyes than her daughter could understand. She felt as if her entire body had been scraped empty from the inside out. Every breath was a chore, and even blinking sent fresh waves of pain radiating through her core.

"Mom!" gasped Nadyra. Her relief was unmistakable. She gently stroked the hair away from Erissa's face while leaning over to kiss her forehead.

The Afyr turned her head toward the commotion to her left. Their small elven savior was backpedaling as fast as her legs would allow, but she was quickly losing the ability to keep up with the demon's frantic pace.

"Help me up," said Erissa. Her voice was no longer her own. It sounded hollow and distant in her ears; a faint echo of what she used to be.

"But–"

"Help me up!" insisted Erissa.

Siscci finally caught hold of the mask and ripped it free of Sylk's face. Tiny bits of skin went with it, leaving little red dots of exposed tissue in its wake. She hissed in delight as she raised the mask to her own face and put it on.

Sylk was thrown to the side by the force of Siscci's tug on the mask. Cold air greeted the myriad tiny wounds on her face as she caught her footing and turned back toward the creature. Siscci followed quickly with a backhand that landed directly in the center of Sylk's chest. The blow knocked her to the ground, prone and vulnerable.

Erissa reached her feet and leaned heavily on Nadyra for support. She stumbled toward the ongoing conflict as fast as her feeble body would allow. As Siscci's backhand knocked Sylk to the ground, the Afyr pointed to the dagger on the ground, and indicated that Nadyra should hand it to her.

Sylk laid on the ground for a moment, unable to breathe. Her heart felt as if it were about to explode, and her lungs simply would not cooperate. All she could do was panic when Siscci reached down and picked her up by the throat.

Erissa shoved Nadyra away when they reached the back of the demon. As the foul creature held Sylk in the air and started removing its mask to feed, Erissa used what remained of her failing energy to drive the dagger into the demon's side, right between the ribs on its left side.

Siscci howled in pain, dropped Sylk and the mask instinctively, and spun to face its unseen foe. She grabbed Erissa; pure, unadulterated hatred rolling out of her in heated waves.

Still struggling to breathe, Sylk stood up and took a few hurried steps forward. As the demon began to feed on Erissa, she quickly pulled the dagger free and returned it to the demon's body with as much force as she could muster. Siscci gasped one last time and fell to the ground atop Erissa; the dagger protruding from the base of its skull, driven in with both hands like Sylk had done to the demon feeding on Jareth.

∴ ∴ ∴

SYLK FELL to her knees, coughing and spitting up specks of blood. As she regained her ability to breathe, Nadyra tried desperately to pull her mother free of the demonic corpse. Erissa was no longer moving or breathing.

When Sylk had finally composed herself, she got up and walked over to Nadyra. She knelt beside the girl and calmly placed a hand on her shoulder.

"She's gone," she whispered. The words were hard to produce through the pain in her throat and the fresh blood filling her mouth.

Rather than attempting to talk again, she gently nudged Nadyra away from Erissa with her hand and pulled the woman's body free. Once Nadyra and her mother were a safe distance away, Sylk returned to the demonic corpse, knelt in front of it and wedged its head between her knees.

She rocked the dagger back and forth with both hands, widening the wound and creating better separation between the vertebrate in her spine. Afterward, she pulled the dagger free and began cutting the head the rest of the way free.

When the head finally popped free, she stood and walked toward the burning church and tossed it in. Nadyra gave her a concerned look when she proceeded around the church into the field beyond. Once there, she found the other demon's corpse and repeated the process.

After she had thrown both heads into the flames, Sylk promptly collapsed from exhaustion and allowed herself to sleep.

PURPOSE

Ris'Anyu, Amaethur 19th, 575 of the 1st Era

HEN SYLK woke up, she was lying on a bedroll on the far side of the road. Nadyra was holding her head in her lap, gently stroking the stubble on her scalp. Several armed men were digging through the debris across the road, talking among themselves.

"H... how?" whispered Sylk.

"They showed up this morning; said they saw the smoke from Errenfall to the north," answered Nadyra as quietly as she could.

"Your mother?" asked Sylk.

"Two men buried her for me."

Sylk tried to move her right hand up to rub her neck, but found it shackled to her left. She looked up at Nadyra with concern in her eyes.

"They want to arrest you. I tried to explain that you saved me, but they wouldn't listen," whispered Nadyra.

The familiar feeling of panic washed over her. She had saved the world and was about to be punished for her efforts. She quickly glanced around, hoping to find a way out. Nadyra interrupted her train of thought.

"It's okay. I managed to grab one of their keys when they weren't looking. I was just waiting for you to wake up," she whispered, smiling.

Sylk nodded back, her panic slowly fading.

They waited patiently for the men to be too distracted to notice and then slipped behind the row of shacks and outhouses. The only thing the men found later was a pair of shackles lying in the brush.

.·. .·. .·.

THE PAIR stumbled through the woods and found Aggie's cabin. It was hidden enough that they decided to stay while Sylk recovered from the fight. Over the next few days, Nadyra tended to her every need, and even read aloud from Aggie's old journals to pass the time. She insisted that Sylk not try to speak until she felt healthy.

A week later, Sylk woke to the smell of dawnfry. She rubbed the sleep from her eyes and walked out to join her young friend. She was quite surprised to see the entire table covered with food.

"I... thank you?" said Sylk as she took her seat. "Did you cook *everything*?"

"It's nice that you have your voice back. You have such a pretty voice," said Nadyra gleefully. "And yes. You seemed almost fit enough to leave yesterday, and this was all about to spoil. I figured why not have a little celebration feast before we hit the road?"

"We?" Sylk wasn't sure what the child was getting at, or if she was ready to care for someone else full time.

"Yes, 'we'. Wherever you're heading, I'm coming with you."

"Oh you are, are you?" teased Sylk.

"Try and stop me!" joked Nadyra as she sat the last plate of fried meat down and joined her at the table.

"I don't know if I'm the right person for you to live with. I don't have a home."

"Well, where are *we* going then?"

"I... I was a slave. I got caught up in all of this, and now it's over. But... I learned a few things in the process. I don't want to be a slave anymore, and I don't want to live in fear. Furthermore, I don't want to sit idly by while others suffer as I did."

"So, what are *we* going to do about it?"

"I am going to put an end to those who treat people like property; like things to be bought and sold. Starting with Samuel."

"Samuel?"

"He's the man that sold me to Johorr. He should be in his forties now, if he's still alive. I hope he's enjoyed his life, because he doesn't have much more of it."

"What will we do after that?"

"Stop with the 'we'. I'm not right for you."

"Who else do I have? Do you plan to drop me off at some orphanage? Might as well brand me a slave yourself. Do you know how they treat half-elves in Lothenheim?"

"You're much more talkative than when I first met you."

"Not so much. I just didn't know you. I was at the top of my class at Schallenhall in Lothenheim. It was quite prestigious. The only reason kids left me alone is I helped them with their work."

"Well, I don't have any specific plans after Samuel. So, 'we' aren't doing anything."

"What about the man that raped my mother?"

Sylk nearly choked on her food. "Are you serious?"

"I've known for a while. It upset mom to talk about, so I pretended I didn't. I've thought about it often; what I would do with him if I ever found him. I mean, sure, without his actions I wouldn't exist, but still... no woman should ever have to endure what my mother did."

Sylk considered for a moment and then decided she liked having company. Company that could share the load, and perhaps teach her to read. "Fine. I have a deal for you. I only know a few written words; not nearly enough to get by on my own. You teach me what you learned in Schallenhall, and I'll help you find the men that attacked your mother."

"It's a deal!" Nadyra squealed.

"We do have one problem, though."

"What's that?"

"They're going to be looking for me. I can't walk around freely in Tellrindos now, and certainly can't go by my real name. I've heard of bounties being passed around the fiefdoms. Delivering on one is a quick way to earn favor from the Kingdom."

"Then we need new names."

"And a new look. I've heard of wizards who can change your appearance; even your race," she mused. "I wish we still had the mask. I could get by with that for a ti-"

"This mask?" interrupted Nadyra as she presented it.

"Where did you-"

"I picked it up and put it in my tunic when I saw the men coming. Wouldn't do anyone any good just sitting on a shelf in Lothenheim. Besides... I owe you everything."

Sylk leaned over and hugged Nadyra more firmly than she'd hugged anyone in decades.

"We'll think of a new name for both of us. Dad talked about a wizard who travels the south that might help with how you look. I think his name was Mordechai. Maybe we could find him?"

"Sounds like a plan. Let's eat our fill and get out of this gods-forsaken Kingdom before something *else* climbs out of the ground to eat us," said Sylk.

SYLK

Ris'Kitthu, Arran'Hael 27th, 635 of the 1st Era

A SINGLE TEAR cascaded down her cheek as the pyre was engulfed in flame. Dozens of women stood around the wooden platform, each dressed in flowing, black silk. It'd been decades since they fled Tellrindos, and she always knew the day would come when Nadyra would part from her presence. That knowledge hadn't made her departure any easier.

It seemed somewhat ironic that news of trouble in Tellrindos would arrive on the same day as her adopted child's passing. The scroll in her hand spoke of an ancient race of subterranean elves raiding the village of Belaigne and stealing children; something she could not abide.

The town guard was useless, as it was in most civil centers. Peopled by those seeking fame, or an easy meal, they did little to protect those in need. The true work was left to the heroes; those that branded themselves adventurers and traveled from place to place in search of riches or glory.

She was neither.

Fame was something she avoided. Those who spoke her name often did so in fear. Everyone else was either oblivious to her existence—which she preferred—or seeking her assistance.

Gold, too, was inconsequential to her. There was a time when she pursued wealth, but those days had long since passed. Coin came with the territory, but wasn't her motivation. The joy she got from riches was fleeting. She'd learned that the hard way, many decades earlier.

Her organization took the jobs that others feared or found distasteful. That was its purpose. That was why she created it. Her agents only took jobs that aligned with her motivations and beliefs. Everything else was off limits.

Missing children, presumably taken by raiders in the night? Local residents too afraid to act? As long as one didn't care *how* the job was done, the Hands of Death was the organization to contact. Just such a job was begging to be taken, right back in the place where her journey once began...

...the place where Sylk first earned her name.

PRONUNCIATION GUIDE

Afyr	-	äh-fēr
Ayr'Thugohn	-	air-thoo-gôn
Dynar	-	die-där
Ekthri	-	ehk-thrē
Siscci	-	sĭssē
Sylk	-	sĭlk
Tellrindos		tell-rĭn-dôss

MONTHS

1	Luthentyr	- loo-thĭn-tēr	Winter
2	Djacenta	- d-jä-sĭn-tä	Winter
3	Brighanfjor	- brĭg-än-f-yor	Winter/Spring
4	Nyevantyr	- nyev-än-tēr	Winter/Spring
5	Caer'Nuun	- k-air-noon	Spring
6	Gwyddinfyr	- g-wĭd-dĭn-fēr	Spring
7	Bloedden'Vasche	- blud-ĭn-vä-sh	Spring/Summer
8	Aiengust	- aīn-gust	Summer
9	Danufyr	- dănoo-fēr	Summer
10	Oghenfall	- ôg-ĭn-fall	Summer/Fall
11	Arran'Hael	- air-ran-hāl	Fall
12	Amaethur	- ä-mā-thur	Fall
13	Ahr'Antaerwyn	- ärr-änt-air-wĭn	Fall/Winter

DAYS OF WEEK

1	Ris'Anyu	- rĭss-än-yoo
2	Ris'Nammlil	- rĭss-näm-lĭl
3	Ris'Kitthu	- rĭss-kĭt-thoo
4	Ris'Gaula	- rĭss-gä-oo-lä
5	Ris'Uttyr	- rĭss-oo-tēr
6	Ris'Enliss	- rĭss-ĭnlĭss